SECRETS AND LIES

a Claire Callahan mystery

P.H. TURNER

Summit Peak Publishing

NOTE FROM THE AUTHOR:

This book is a work of fiction. The names, characters, places, and incidents are products of the writer's imagination or have been used fictitiously and are not to be construed as real. Any resemblance to persons, living or dead, actual events, locale or organizations is entirely coincidental. The author does not have any control over and does not assume any responsibility for third-party websites or their content.

Published in the United States of America
Summit Peak Publishing

To Marcia, Matthew, and Alison for your love and support.
Always.

CHAPTER ONE

JESSE DROVE THE STOLEN TOYOTA UP TO THE GATE, rolled down the window and let the smell of pizza waft out of the car into the crisp fall night. With the Big Pies sign on the roof and the company gimme cap jammed low over his forehead, he was sure the guard in the hut would wave him through with no questions.

Sure enough, the guy barely glanced up from his laptop and buzzed the barricade arm up.

Jesse drove into the exclusive neighborhood, ogling the houses and looking for the address he'd torn out of a phonebook.

He slowed at a Children at Play traffic sign, careful to obey all the laws even if dark came early in the fall evenings, and the kids were all inside waiting for their dinner. Well-bred, tidy kids. No bicycles in the driveways or skateboards kicked up in the grass. Their parents would soon be tucking them in their beds claiming they didn't need to leave a light on. There were no bogeymen in this neighborhood.

Another block and he pulled into the circle drive of

781 Boulder Creek. The old car gave a groaning moan and shuddered to a stop.

Sounds like the freakin' power steering pump is on its last leg.

He headed up the front walk, stopping to tweak the crotch of the uniform pants bunching between his legs. Too bad the guy he'd killed for it hadn't been twenty pounds heavier and three inches taller.

Jesse held the gun behind his right leg, and in his left hand, he held the red thermal pizza delivery bag where anyone looking could easily see it. He stood under the porch light and rang the doorbell with his left elbow.

A middle-aged balding man glanced out one of the side panes of glass. Jesse waggled the bag and smiled. The older man frowned and opened the door.

Jesse dropped the pizza bag, shoving the Smith & Wesson right in the guy's face. Jesse moved forward, pushing him back into the house, keeping the gun right off the tip of his nose. He kicked the heavy oak door shut with his foot, then shot the man in the shoulder. The gunshot was no louder than a casserole dish hitting a tile floor—he'd put enough rounds through the silencer to be sure the noise wouldn't have the neighbors calling the cops.

The guy fell backward, banging his head on the wall. Then he just lay still.

Jesse stepped over him and ran into the living room.

Morgan Tutwiler rushed through a door yelling, "Hawkins, what in the hell is going on?"

He stopped dead in his tracks when he saw the gun.

"No, please —"

Jesse aimed at his chest and squeezed the trigger twice. *Thunk-thunk.*

Tutwiler slumped to the floor like a bag of wet laundry.

Jesse stood over Tutwiler's body, waiting for the feelings to come—relief, joy . . . something.

Damn it! Where is my freakin' happy?

Jesse ran to the front door.

Hawkins was alert, his eyes following as he ran past.

Jesse yanked open the front door, grabbed the red bag off the porch and fast-walked to the Toyota. He tossed the pizza bag on the passenger seat and stuck the gun under the front seat.

His pants were so tight he had to half sit up in the driver's seat to dig the keys out of his pocket. When he turned the key in the ignition, he heard *ruh ruh ruh.*

Was the damn car even going to start?

He cranked the key in the ignition and stomped hard on the accelerator. The car sputtered and turned over.

His heart pounding, sweating like a racehorse, he forced himself to drive slowly through the neighborhood to the guard hut. He wiped the sweat off his face with his sleeve and smiled when he idled at the gate.

The guard glanced up from diddling with his phone and waved him through.

He thought he'd made a clean getaway until a distracted woman in a minivan ran the stop sign outside Tutwiler's neighborhood, nearly broadsiding him.

Jesse stomped on the brakes and swerved toward the curb. The brakes squealed, and the old rust-bucket popped the curb, shuddering to a stop with the front wheels in the grass. The gun slid out from under the seat coming to rest under his feet. Fortunately, the engine didn't die.

The minivan-driving Mom with a row of little heads in the back seat shot him the finger and sped off.

Jesse stuck the gun back under the seat, backed off

the curb, and drove the speed limit to an abandoned warehouse south of the truck stop on Interstate 70.

It was one of dozens in a deserted industrial complex. Squatters had been living in the warehouse when he found the place. He chased them off, piled their sleeping bags in a heap and set fire to them. He'd spent a couple of nights watching the place, and they hadn't come back.

The warehouse was dark except for the few panes of broken glass up along the roofline letting in moonlight. He parked in the back corner, well out of sight from any cop driving by making his rounds. There were plenty of abandoned crates and machinery. He'd moved them around until he had his little hidey hole.

He unstrapped the Big Pies sign from the top of the car and threw it in the backseat. Amped up on adrenaline, he changed into his clothes in between bites of pizza. He threw the uniform in the back seat, remembered to get the gun, and left the keys in the ignition.

For a guy who had never murdered anyone, he decided he'd done a damn fine job. It had all worked like he planned. The Big Pies guy showed up at the truck with a pie, the silencer had worked like a champ, and back in the dark by the dumpsters, no one had seen him strip the dead man. Finding and killing Tutwiler was easier than a deer hunt.

Jesse stuffed the gun in his waistband and walked over to the corner of the warehouse to take a piss. It was a two-mile walk east to the truck stop's lot where he'd left his pickup.

His camping gear, plenty of food, and his rifle were stashed in the camper shell. If he showed at the ranch in a couple of days with a mud-spattered truck and his clothes smelling of wood smoke, Gus would believe he'd been camping in the Arapaho National Forest. No reason for anyone to suspect he'd made a little side-trip to Denver and killed a man.

The lights of the truck stop shone up ahead of him. He bushwhacked through a vacant lot bordering the east side of the parking lot. No one noticed when he stepped into the lot by the diesel pumps. The lot was too busy with hungry truckers rolling in for gas and grub.

He didn't draw a second glance when he crossed the pavement to his pickup, unlocked it and drove away.

He took the Interstate north. He did worry a bit about not killing the man Tutwiler called Hawkins on the way out of the house, but he couldn't shoot him. Not with him just lying there staring at him, waiting for it. He didn't have a beef with Tutwiler's hired hand.

Most likely, it'd all turn out just fine.

He cruised into the parking lot of an all-night convenience store. A couple of gang bangers loitered out front smoking and drinking beer.

Jesse parked by a dumpster overflowing with trash. He dropped the gun in a plastic grocery bag and tossed the sack in the bin.

He put the pickup in gear and continued driving north. He rehashed the night's work, looking for any mistakes he'd made.

Hawkins wasn't going to be able to describe him. His attention was on the gun. But even if the guy took in everything, Jesse was nothing special to look at, and he'd worn the gimme cap. He'd left fingerprints, but the cops could search their databases until the moon turned blue and they wouldn't find him in a computer.

Yeah, it was going be fine.

When he saw the exit to the Arapaho wilderness area, Jesse quit thinking about the shooting. He was going camping.

The dirt-packed forest road was one lane wide with turnarounds every two or three miles. Ten miles into the wilderness, he rocked over a ridgeline and dropped down deep into the backcountry.

An hour later, he was in his tent listening to the rain. That soon turned to sleet. Then, heavy wet snow. Snow that might be a foot deep by morning.

Colder than a witch's teat in a brass bra, he hunkered down spending a miserable night. He pulled the sleeping bag over his head to trap his warm breath and thought about her.

His whole life flushed down the crapper when she walked out the door.

He missed her something fierce. Did she miss him a teeny bit? Did she even think about him?

What would she think when she found out Tutwiler was dead?

She'd know it was him. Know he'd done it for her. No one else would have killed him for her.

Maybe she'll come see me.

He tried to sleep, but the cold settled so deeply into his bones, he thought they'd crack when he stood.

Come daylight, he peeked out the tent flap. A couple of inches of snow lay on the ground, and windblown drifts were piling up on the north side of the tent. Nothing to do but head to the ranch.

Jesse broke camp and threw his gear in the back of the pickup. With one foot on the brake, he revved the motor to warm the cab faster. He wanted pavement under his tires and a big cup of hot coffee in his hands. It took him nearly three hours to reach the paved road.

The storm would make his story more believable. Snow packed up in the wheel wells and muddy side panels would back up his story he'd gotten caught in a storm. No one would suspect he'd gone to Denver.

The storm was well north and west of the city, and with the wind blowing the storm their way, the hands would be too busy dropping hay for the cattle to pay him any attention.

He pulled into a gas station and topped off the tank before going inside for coffee. He hung around for a minute or two hoping the clerk would turn on the television. When the clerk showed no sign of turning the set on, Jesse left disappointed. The radio in his pickup hadn't worked in years. He had put a brand-new coat hanger in the antenna hole before he left home, but still, nothing.

Two miles up the road he took the ramp onto the Interstate. Traffic moved slowly in the light snow, and then all the northbound lanes turned into a parking lot. Row after row of taillights. Sirens and flashing lights came up from behind and shot past him on the shoulder moving fast to the accident blocking the road ahead.

Traffic was stalled the better part of an hour before two lanes were cleared and he crept past the accident scene.

Tutwiler's murder would have to be all over the news. She might be reading it in the papers right this minute or watching it on television. Maybe she was reaching for the phone to call him.

When he was clear of the jam up of cars, he whipped around a semi, hauling way too fast on the wet road. He wished he had a cell phone. He'd call her if he did.

Sheets of dry snow blew across the Interstate, and he slowed to less than 30 miles an hour. Riding in a slow-moving stream of traffic, Jesse had time to think.

He regretted killing the delivery guy. The guy looked so damned surprised when he'd shot him, but Jesse needed the uniform and car, and the way Jesse figured it, the driver didn't die in vain. Innocent men laid down their lives every day for something bigger than themselves.

Tutwiler needed to be killed. He was a lying bastard. Cheated everyone on every deal he worked. Even when the bridge he built collapsed, his attorney off-loaded the blame onto everyone but him.

She got caught up in Tutwiler's mess, and he hurt her. Jesse did what a man does for his womenfolk. He righted the scales. It'd taken him some time to get the job done right. He'd read every newspaper article for the past year on Tutwiler. The ranch's dial-up connection really slowed him down, but he'd even printed some and made a little book of important things he'd need to know. Just like he studied the habits of deer before he went stalking. Not much difference in preparing for a deer hunt and a manhunt.

It was late when he turned off the county road and rolled up to the ranch gate. The wind tore at his coat when he pushed the gate back on its hinges. Icy blue clouds rolled off the horizon and raced across the sky. The storm was coming, and it was bringing snow.

He pulled the pickup up around to the side door of the ranch house. He could sure do with some of Frieda's cooking. When his grandpa died, she and Gus took him in and ran the ranch.

He came through the back door into the kitchen. Frieda was washing the supper dishes in the sink.

"That you Jesse?" Freida asked without looking up.

"Yeah. Something smells good." Jesse toed off his muddy boots and walked in his sock feet to the stove. He lifted the lid off a big stew pot, and the kitchen filled with the scent of boiled beef.

Gus walked in. "Got hit with the storm, didn't you?"

"Miserable out there," Jesse said. "There's more

snow than I've ever seen in the Arapaho this early in the fall, and the storm chased me all the way home."

"Weather Service says it's going to be a bad one, high winds and at least a foot of snow," Gus said.

"You eat it while it's warm," Frieda said. She set a bowl of beef and mushy vegetables in front of Jesse.

"Thanks," Jesse said.

"I wouldn't let you go hungry." She patted his shoulder.

Gus reached over and turned on the radio.

Jesse tried not to look eager. He had to look as surprised as Gus and Frieda when the news of Tutwiler came on. After the weather, and the commodities report and the cattle futures, the announcer read the news story of Tutwiler's murder.

Frieda whirled around and looked at Gus. He held up his hand to keep her quiet until the reporter finished the story.

Frieda snapped the dish towel on the counter top. "I told you that business wasn't finished. That man was pure evil, brought nothing but pain and misery to everyone around him. She'll be a suspect. You know she will."

"She doesn't have anything to worry about," Gus said.

She would be a suspect? He never meant to cause her trouble.

"She's never been who you thought she was," Frieda said. "A conniving woman. You know what I'm talking about. Old man, you were always blind about her."

Gus slapped his palm down on the table. "Enough, woman. You never liked her, doesn't mean she's a bad person."

Frieda turned her back on Gus and slammed the

skillet in the sink. She stomped out of the kitchen and up the stairs.

Gus headed to his recliner in the living room.

Jesse shoved in one last mouthful of food. He unplugged the radio, followed Gus into the living room, and plugged it in there.

Gus popped up the footrest on the recliner. "Don't worry about Frieda's moods. Remember when you used to tie a string around one leg of a June bug, and he'd buzz around like crazy? That's the way to handle an angry woman. Let her buzz at the end of her string until she's wore out. She'll come around."

Jesse fiddled with the radio trying to find another station and more news, but he could only pick up the AM station they had been listening to.

"Don't fret none about her being a suspect," Gus said. "She'll come out of this okay. You hear me? Don't be worrying."

Jesse mumbled "Yes" only to keep Gus quiet, so he could hear the radio.

The news reported on the storm and then the station went live to a play by play of the local six-man football team.

Jesse turned the set off. "I'm going up to bed."

Upstairs in his room, he crawled into bed and watched the snow pound against his window.

Why hadn't she called?

He'd done what a man did for a woman he loved. Any man who didn't protect his womenfolk was worthless as horse apples.

CHAPTER TWO

CLAIRE CALLAHAN TYPED THE LAST WORDS OF THE LAST paragraph in her final report, tears threatening. This child custody case was worse than typical – to her, they were all bad—and tore Claire's heart out. She clicked *Send* without even bothering to proofread it like she usually did. All she wanted was to go home and watch Netflix and eat leftover pizza.

She shut down her computer and sprinted to the elevator to the garage.

As a young and eager private investigator for the prestigious law firm of Marsh and Whitley, sometimes the job broke her heart, sometimes it put her in danger, sometimes it frustrated her . . . but it never bored her. That would be a deal breaker.

Claire unlocked Bug, mentally crossed her fingers hoping he would start and pulled out of the parking garage. Bug couldn't do better than to putter-put in the slow lane of the Interstate, but the poor thing was over twenty years old. In car-years, that was like a hundred. He had a new set of tires and a shiny new black paint job, but he needed a new motor, and his asthmatic heater was going to have to be replaced before the Denver winter set in.

She did her best to ignore the rusted-out holes in the passenger side floorboards—holes big enough to see the asphalt whiz by on a sunny day. The little guy needed more restoration than she had money.

Rafe accused her of being nuts for pouring money into the "heap," but Bug was nearly a classic. And besides, a car payment wasn't in the budget.

Detective Rafe Brewster shared the same goal she had: To see that justice was done.

They had nearly ruined a perfectly good working relationship by having a dinner date. Fortunately, by the time the bill arrived, they came to their senses, went Dutch, and agreed the evening had been too awkward to ever bring up again.

She felt the emotional pull between them—maybe more of a tug, an occasional *what if?* He had what any gal would want in a man, but how often do you find the perfect workmate? They were comfortable with each other and had common experiences, like their disastrous love lives.

He was divorced. Her love life was littered with a string of three-date experiences—she could hardly call relationships—and a one year-long engagement that died of sheer tedium. She figured The One might still turn up—you never knew about these things.

She exited the freeway into south central Denver and drove toward the first home she ever owned. Well, almost owned. The bank had a hand in the deal, but the small duplex with one bedroom and a tiny extra space she used as an office made her feel happy every time she turned into the driveway.

From the street, it was no eye catcher. Built in the 1960s, it was a red brick rectangle with two front doors, hers on the right and painted the blue-gray of a Denver summer storm. She wished it had a carport. But it was a plus she didn't have neighbors on the other side.

The interior needed a new coat of paint and new floors, but for right now, nothing new was in her budget, certainly not the gorgeous furniture she drooled over watching HGTV.

She turned on South Zuni street dreaming of the good bottle of Riesling in the fridge and binge watching the rest of *Homeland.* She was two blocks from home when her phone rang.

She checked the screen. Kirwin. This was not going to be good news.

"Hey, Pigeon."

And when he used her childhood nickname, he wanted something.

After twenty years without a word, he'd turned up at her office last year. He bunked in her tiny apartment for a couple nights. Then one evening, he went out for a pack of smokes and never came back.

He was on the other end of the phone. *What now?*

"Hi, Kirwin."

Her parents dumped her on Grandma Callie when she was six. By the time she was seven, she'd quit waiting at the window for them to come back.

"I got some trouble," Kirwin said. "I'm on the porch at your place. Your office gave me your new address. Can I sleep on your sofa? I won't stay long."

He's broke again and needs a roof over his head.

Maybe he heard her sigh. Or maybe her lack of a response caused him to fill in the blanks.

"Pigeon, I'm sober now."

Not in a million years.

She wrestled with what to do. Put your feet in the right place and stand firm was hard for her when dealing with Kirwin—an unemployed alcoholic. She couldn't even get her mouth to say "Dad".

But without Kirwin, there would be no her . . . so did she owe him? Or was taking him in making him dependent? An answer to a question that complex wasn't coming in the next few seconds before she had to decide whether to turn into the driveway, or just keep driving.

"I'm running late," she said. "The key is in the fake white rock in the flower bed on the south side of the front door. Make yourself at home."

She hung up and headed to the gym. With luck, Kirwin would be asleep by the time she got home.

Her phone rang again.

Uh-oh.

Founding partner Charles Marsh never called after hours unless something was urgent. She pressed the button and before she could even say hello—

"Claire, Morgan Tutwiler is dead," he said.

She nearly drove Bug over the curb. "What? What happened?"

"He was shot to death in his home. How soon can you get over there?"

Her phone beeped. She looked at the screen. An incoming call from Rafe. Suddenly, she was more popular than a drunk Homecoming Queen. She let it go to voicemail.

"I'm on my way," she told Marsh. "Is there anything else you can tell me?"

"His daughter is flying in."

She did an illegal U-turn and headed to Tutwiler's house. She could find the place blindfolded. A year ago, her job had been to keep him safe.

"Amanda's our new client," Marsh said. "She inherits it all except a bequest to Hawkins and another to the cook. I'm depending on you to help her through this whole shitstorm—you know the headlines coming. 'Most Hated Man in Denver Murdered, Daughter Inherits.' You can bet your ass that's the morning news lead. Amanda's going to require some of that kid-glove handling you're good at doling out. I'll text you her arrival time. Pick her up and get started." He hung up.

Resuming her duties as chief hand-holder to Amanda Tutwiler wasn't a role she relished. Morgan Tutwiler had been their rainmaker. Losing his business would hurt the firm's bottom line. She'd fall in line, do her job and try to keep the new heiress happy, but she didn't have to enjoy it.

A twenty-one-year-old Boston University student as the new rainmaker. Claire could hardly take it in. *Wonder how much she's changed in the last year?*

Claire returned Rafe's call.

"Hey, Morgan Tutwiler's been murdered," Rafe said. "I'm on my way to his house."

"Me too. Marsh just called me."

"Hawkins Reynolds called it in. He's wounded."

"Is he going to make it?"

"Hope so. He's an eyewitness," Rafe said. "How far out are you?"

"I just passed the exit to the Country Club. Be there in a minute."

"You'll get there before me. Two patrol officers are there. Herbst and Keller. Wait with them," Rafe said before he hung up.

She turned into Tutwiler's neighborhood. His gated community was built around the golf course of the Denver Country Club. The lights were on in the guard hut, but the guard wasn't there. The barricade arm was in the raised position.

Marsh & Whitley had represented Morgan Tutwiler

for years. Their client made a fortune with a conglomerate of businesses operating under the name of Tutwiler Industries. A year ago, he had survived death threats, a vicious divorce, a criminal trial, and a civil suit.

Tonight, his luck had run out.

She drove into the cul-de-sac to Tutwiler's highly stylized Tudor house. Showcasing elaborate stonework, dormers, gables, and a porte-cochère, the mansion sat like an island of old England in the middle of the Queen City of the Plains.

A cruiser was parked haphazardly in the circle in front of the house, its flashers bouncing blue and red lights off the houses. A crowd of looky-loos gathered in front of Tutwiler's home, and a crew from a local television station was cranking up the microwave antenna on their van. An ambulance in the driveway had its rear doors open.

Claire pulled in next to the curb in front of a neighbor's house and parked. She glanced at her watch, and jotted the time, seven-forty, in her notebook.

She walked toward Officer Nicole Keller, who was standing in Tutwiler's yard watching the crowd gather in the street.

Nicole was a tall brunette with the athletic grace of a dedicated runner and an ambitious cop. Claire and Nicole trained together for the Denver 5K, Claire's first and last marathon.

Rafe pulled up in his police-issue Ford Escape as Nicole was telling Claire that she and her partner had answered the 911 call a little after 7 PM.

Rafe was talking to Nicole almost before he got out of his vehicle. "Push the perimeter all the way across the street, and get those bystanders moved," he said. "Then, start interviewing the crowd. And where's the gate guard?"

Nicole pointed to a man sitting by himself on the curb. "Over there. His name's Hal Huber."

"Keep him isolated and where you can see him," Rafe said. "And when backup comes, set up a command center inside the perimeter."

"Yes sir," Nicole said.

Rafe turned to Claire. "Let's go."

She fell in beside him. They walked up the drive to the front door.

Rafe held his badge out to a middle-aged officer whose nameplate identified him as Doug Herbst. "Detective Brewster and Ms. Callahan."

Herbst nodded. "My partner and I arrived at twelve minutes after seven. Officer Keller secured the perimeter. I went into the house and found two victims. Hawkins Reynolds is wounded and in the entryway. The dead man is in the living room. Reynolds identified him as Morgan Tutwiler."

"Stay on the door and keep a log of who goes in and out," Rafe said as he slipped on shoe covers and gloves.

Claire snatched a pair of each and pulled them on, then followed Rafe into the foyer.

It was an elegant entrance into a stunning house. Long and narrow, the corridor had large oil paintings hung on the walls, white marble flooring, and was lit with a pair of matching chandeliers.

Hawkins Reynolds lay propped up against a bloodstained wall three feet from the front door. Two emergency medical technicians were laying out gear.

Claire and Rafe approached the victim, careful not to step in the bloody footprints leading out the front door.

Rafe knelt by Reynolds. "I'm Detective Brewster. Can you tell me what happened?"

Hawkins Reynolds looked up at Claire. Sweat was pouring off his face, but he offered a grim smile. "Claire . . ."

She squatted beside him. "Hey Hawkins, looks like you're in good hands. What happened."

"I, uh . . ." He winced when the EMT stuck a needle in his arm. "A pizza delivery boy was at the door, and I opened it. Mr. Tutwiler —" his voice broke. "He'd be alive if I'd kept the door shut." He looked at Claire with woeful eyes. "We didn't order a pizza."

"What did the man look like?" Rafe asked.

The EMT looked at Rafe. "You got one minute, and then we're out of here." He pressed sterile packing to the wound in Hawkins' shoulder.

Hawkins groaned. "He . . .uh . . . oh God, that hurts. I don't know, ordinary looking. Dark hair, white guy . . . I didn't recognize him. I know that."

"He's done," the EMT rose and stood by Rafe. "You can talk to him at the hospital."

Rafe asked, "Did the guy say anything?"

Hawkins shook his head.

"Sir," the EMT said to his patient, "we're going to get you out of here."

The EMTs loaded Hawkins on the stretcher and took him out the door.

After the medical personnel were out of earshot, Claire said, "The killer had two chances to kill Hawkins and didn't—when he came in and when he left."

Rafe walked toward the living room. "Yeah, was the guy stupid or did he have a reason? Let's see the body before the ME arrives."

A floor-to-ceiling fireplace would have been the room's focal point if Tutwiler's body hadn't been sprawled by the hearth, blood pooled on the gold rug under him. The room was cluttered with dark, heavy furniture and bric-a-brac.

Tutwiler lay on his back, his white bathrobe gaping open to reveal two bullet wounds in his chest. His legs were spread about eighteen inches, his feet bare, and his hands flung out from his body. His face was frozen in an expression of mild surprise.

Rafe bent over the body and with a pen pulled the robe further aside. Tutwiler's gray chest hair grew in sparse tufts down the center of his chest toward his groin. The curly hair around his nipples was bloodied. "Two bullets placed three inches apart. The killer was either close to him or a fine shot." Rafe stood up and turned in a circle getting a feel for the room. "Three ways in, from the foyer, the back French doors, and a hallway."

Claire pointed to the short hallway off the living room. There was light seeping into the hall from an open doorway. "His office is down that hall. It looks like he came in here from there. And unless he's lying on it, he didn't bring a gun with him."

"Did he keep guns in the house?"

"A year ago, he did. There was a gun cabinet in his office with a long gun and a couple of pistols, and he kept a loaded pistol in his desk drawer."

Rafe turned his head to glance toward the front door. "He's what? Twelve feet from the foyer? Hell of a decision to come unarmed to a gun fight."

Heavy car doors slammed, and there were voices at the front door.

"Irv's here," Rafe said.

Dr. Irv Iverson strode in smelling like cigar smoke and carrying a heavy black bag. Iverson had a reputation for being short-tempered and territorial. True to his reputation, he snapped at Rafe. "The body's mine."

"Good evening, Dr. Iverson," Rafe said. "The crime scene's mine and the body is part of the crime scene. How about we call a truce tonight?"

"Hey, Brewster," a man's voice yelled from outside. "Tell this clown to let me in."

Rafe turned so he could see the doorway. "Lensman Zhang, the photog," he said to Herbst.

Lensman had earned his nickname by being the best. He brushed past Herbst and carried his equipment cases into the foyer and went to work setting up markers and a reference ruler by the footprints.

On the heels of Lensman's arrival, the crime scene team came in.

Iverson was squatting by the body unpacking his case.

Claire caught Rafe's attention and pointed toward Tutwiler's office.

He nodded, and she walked away.

The office was out of the line of sight of the crime team in the living room. Since she wore gloves, she made herself at home.

She opened the top right drawer of the desk. There was his handgun. She shook her head. He would have had a chance if he had taken it with him.

She closed it and flipped through an open file folder on his desk and saw it was full of purchase orders for the brew pubs he owned.

His screen saver brightened when she touched his laptop, but no windows were open, and the machine was password protected. She'd have to wait until the cops took it apart and then maybe she could wheedle out of Rafe whatever they discovered.

She leafed through his files and found folders labeled

accountant, vendors, contracts—nothing she wouldn't expect to see in a home office.

She returned to the living room.

Rafe walked toward her. "Find anything?"

"Gun's in his drawer where he kept it. He has a laptop and it's password protected." She shrugged. "Nothing special about the paper files he was working on."

"We'll dust for prints and pack out his office," Rafe said.

A CSI tech called out to Rafe and held up a spent shell. "He didn't collect all his brass."

Rafe looked at Claire and raised his brows. "Maybe we got lucky and we have prints."

"You better get over here," Iverson said. "You'll want to see this."

They walked over and squatted on their heels by Tutwiler's body.

"Look here," he said "where my finger is." He was probing one of the bullet wounds with a gloved finger.

"The entrance wounds are erythematous, rather than abraded. Means the edges are puffed up and red from the increased capillary flow." He tapped the raised ridge around one of the wounds. "And see the shape of the entry wounds? Not oval, but not round either, and barely sooted with powder. The killer used a silencer."

He looked up at Rafe. "I'd say the killer was less than three feet away when he shot him."

"Time of death?" Rafe asked.

"Less than two hours. Does that fit with your witness's statement?" Iverson said.

Rafe nodded.

Iverson rolled Tutwiler on his side, pulled the robe down and exposing the dead man's back. "You don't seem too surprised about the silencer."

"The neighbors didn't call it in."

Iverson nodded without looking up at Rafe. "See," he pointed. "No exit wounds."

Tutwiler's skin was already taking on a dull blue hue. He'd been dead long enough that the blood pooled to the lowest level of the body. Iverson sat back on his heels. "He hasn't been moved. Backs of the legs show the same lividity." Iverson rolled the body back face up.

He stood, his knees creaking. "He'll be on my table first thing in the morning. Now, get Lensman over here to take his pictures so we can move him to the morgue."

Iverson stood by the body, stripping off his gloves while Lensman got close-ups of Tutwiler's hands, the gunshot residue, and the wounds. He circled the body, firing off pictures from all angles and elevations.

The morgue attendants moved Tutwiler's body out the French doors to the backyard in order to stay clear of the crime scene team working in the entry hall. Once the body was moved, members of the team rolled up the rug Tutwiler died on and carted it out to their van.

Rafe and Claire retreated to the backyard to talk privately.

"The whole setup's odd. Hawkins opens the door to a stranger, the killer leaves him alive," Claire said. "People have learned way too much from watching TV to leave an eyewitness alive."

"Why do you think Hawkins opened the door?" Rafe asked.

"You'll have to tell me how he answers that question when you talk to him at the hospital. It's not just what the killer did that's odd. It's Hawkins, too. He has said he's a veteran. If he did serve, he would have dragged himself over to Tutwiler and rendered aid. And he would have recognized the gun had a silencer on the end of it." She shook her head. "The whole thing is wonky. A year ago, Tutwiler was the most hated man in Denver. Hawkins said they didn't order pizza, so why did he open the door? It makes no sense."

Rafe looked thoughtful. "You're making a pretty solid case that Hawkins was in on it. Find out from that boss of yours if he inherits."

Claire's phone vibrated in her pocket.

Marsh texted: *Amanda arriving midnight on United. Reservation downtown Marriott. You know what to do.*

She texted Marsh: *On it.*

She looked up at Rafe. "That was Marsh telling me when Amanda arrives. Yeah, Hawkins and the cook get small bequests. The rest of the estate goes to Amanda."

"Makes her a prime suspect," Rafe said.

"Why don't we wait until we see her again? Unless she's done a one hundred and eighty-degree turnaround from the milquetoast kid she was a year ago, she couldn't swat a fly."

"She could have hired someone to kill her father," Rafe said.

"Let's get her on the ground and talk to her before we string her up."

Rafe grinned. "Interesting to watch you defend her before you've seen her, yet you're ready to lock up Hawkins."

"No comparison. She was in Boston. Hawkins opened the door, and a killer walked out leaving him alive."

"Or how about this," Rafe said. "Amanda hired a killer and paid Hawkins to let the shooter in. And then Hawkins took a bullet to make it look real."

"Oh yeah, sure. Prove it up," Claire said heading for the door. "I got a few minutes before I have to go. I want to talk to the gate guard."

Hal Huber was still sitting on the curb where Nicole had told him to stay put.

Rafe held up his badge. "Mr. Huber, I have a few questions."

Huber gave the credentials a glance. "Everyone calls me Hal."

"Okay, Hal. Anyone come through the gate tonight who didn't live here?"

"Sure. A guy from Big Pies Pizza came through at six-thirty."

"You're good on the time?" Claire asked.

"I know exactly when he drove through. I keep a log on the laptop. It's part of my job. Six-thirty," Huber repeated.

His timing fit.

"Can you describe the driver?" Rafe asked.

"Do you know how many pizza deliveries I get?" Huber shook his head in bewilderment. "None of these women cook. The teens have the pizza places on speed dial."

"Take your time. Anything will help," Rafe said.

"He had the Pies sign strapped on the top of his car and he was wearing the Big Pies uniform and cap. He wasn't old, I remember that." Huber scratched the stubble on his chin. "White guy for sure, maybe he had brown hair. The cap was jammed down so low it made his ears stick out."

"Anything else?" Rafe asked.

Huber frowned impatiently. "He was just another guy delivering a pizza. I didn't know I'd have to describe him."

"What about the vehicle?"

"It was an old car, white or tan. A Toyota, I think. One of the back taillights was busted out. Dent in the rear on that side . . . right side maybe." He grinned. "I know the plate number began with triple D, my favorite cup size."

Claire pointed to the roof of the guard hut. "We'll need the footage from that camera."

"Don't work. I reported it last week. I got the email I sent the company."

"I'll need to take the laptop," Rafe said.

"It's locked up in the guard hut." Hal handed Rafe the keys.

"What's a good number for you?" Rafe said.

Hal rattled off his number. "Most days, you can find me right here. Unless I lost my job tonight."

They left Hal sitting on the curb.

Rafe called in a BOLO on the car while he and Claire walked over to Officer Keller. Rafe handed Nicole the keys. "There's a laptop in the guard hut. I need you to get it. What did you get from the neighbors?"

Nicole pocketed the keys and looked down at her notes.

"There are four houses in the cul-de-sac. Starting from the east, the first house is the Osborn's. Mr. Osborn and his ten-year-old son were the only two home. They were eating dinner in the back of the house and they couldn't see the street, and the first thing they heard was the sirens.

"Next house is Ms. Beverly Bryant's." She pointed to the house next to Tutwiler's. She's divorced, lives alone, and was upstairs practicing yoga. She said she never knew anything was going on until she came downstairs and saw the cop car." Nicole looked up from her notes and frowned. "She asked a lot of questions about Mr. Reynolds—it was weird."

"Weird how?" Rafe asked.

"Her neighbor had been shot to death, and she

keeps asking if Hawkins—she didn't call him Mr. Reynolds, is going to be all right, and what hospital he went to, and did I see him before the ambulance took him away. Just a bit off considering the circumstances."

Rafe wiped his hand across his mouth. "Did she give you any reason why she has a personal interest in Mr. Reynolds?"

Nicole shook her head

"Okay, good catch, I'll follow up with her. Who lives on the other side of Tutwiler?"

"Joe and Helen Bautista. Both are in their mid-seventies. They were in the backyard grilling, and they said they weren't wearing their hearing aids." She looked up at Rafe. "They're deaf as posts without those hearing aids, and the shrubbery around their property is so thick I couldn't see into the backyard.

"Okay, so the Osborn house and the Bryant house have security cameras, and I told them we'd need to see the footage."

"Thanks. Good work. Get the cards from their cameras and sign for it."

"Sir," Officer Keller said tentatively. "I'd like to be assigned to work on this case. I'm taking the detective exam soon and I need some real-life experience."

Claire could see Rafe was weighing the pros and cons before he said, "I'll put a word in with Captain Beekman."

"Thank you, sir," Nicole said.

Once they were out of earshot, Claire said to Rafe, "Captain Beekman still hasn't filled the open position?"

"No, and she's got a lot of potential. Working with Herbst pulls her off her game. He was busted down to patrol for anger problems. Turns out he was a steroid abuser."

"Did someone upstairs not like Nicole to saddle her with Herbst as a partner?" Claire asked.

"I don't know that anyone has an issue with her. What do you think about the Bryant woman asking about Reynolds?"

"They're about the same age, both single and live next door to each other. Maybe they were friendly, or more than friends." Claire checked the time. "I have to go. After I get Amanda checked into the Marriott, I have Kirwin to deal with, so I'll be up. Text me if anything breaks."

"When did Kirwin show up?"

"A couple of hours ago."

"Better buy him a pack of cigs on your way home." Rafe grinned, then turned serious. "I assume he has money troubles again?"

"Probably."

Rafe ran his hand over his face. "The man needs help." He held up one palm to stop her from interrupting. "I know a psychologist he could talk to."

"I don't know if Kirwin can afford that."

"Kirwin's old enough to be on Medicare and he has his VA benefits. He'll be fine."

"He won't admit he has a problem."

"You're throwing up roadblocks. You have to draw a line in the sand."

Claire put her hands on her hips. "You're saying I enable him?"

"I'm saying Kirwin has all his marbles. He knows he has problems and as long as he has a place to crash, he's going to do what he wants."

Claire wondered if she just got her answer to whether she owed Kirwin or not.

Rafe walked off, saying over his shoulder. "Think about it."

CHAPTER THREE

THE LAST TIME CLAIRE HAD SEEN AMANDA TUTWILER A year ago, the twenty-year-old was running from intense media scrutiny to a new life in Boston.

Now, waiting in arrivals, Claire expected the mousy, overweight young woman to come through the doors skittish of her own shadow.

Instead, after a tap on her shoulder, Claire turned to see a sleek young woman in black leggings, to-die-for thigh-high suede boots and a short sweater dress the color of a gin-soaked olive.

It took Claire a moment to recognize her.

"Hi," Amanda said, running one hand through her hair, now blonde and cut so expertly it fell back in place around her face and cupped under her chin. "How nice for you to meet me." She leaned in and air-kissed close to Claire's ear.

"Welcome home," Claire said. "I'm sorry about your Dad."

Amanda looked sly. "You're surprised at the changes in me."

"You look wonderful," Claire said.

"I should. I've worked on myself for a year. This is the new me, and she isn't trapped under Daddy's thumb." She looked uncomfortable for a moment, then turned and walked toward the escalator to baggage claim. "I guess, I shouldn't have said that. Don't speak ill of the dead and all."

Claire fell into step beside her.

Amanda looked over at Claire as they stepped on the escalator. "I'm not sorry he's dead. I've wished he was dead plenty of times."

"Why don't we continue this conversation in the car?"

"Oh, Claire, you're so antediluvian. It's fine, I didn't kill him."

"It's best if we don't read your conversation in the *Post* in the morning."

Amanda giggled as she stepped off the escalator and turned around to Claire. "You wouldn't have recognized me if I hadn't walked up to you."

She was right. Amanda had shed at least thirty pounds, and while Claire couldn't swear to it, the young lady's nose looked like it had received the attention of a good plastic surgeon. Coupled with the gorgeous hair, the attitude, and the new style of dress, Claire would have walked past her and kept looking for a drab, timid girl with her head tucked on her chest.

The amber light was flashing, and baggage tumbled out of the chute unto the carousel.

Amanda pointed to a set of Louis Vuitton luggage, and Claire hauled off the first one and handed it over. She was quick enough to grab the next without waiting for it to come around again.

Amanda led the way carrying her matching handbag and satchel.

Claire trailed behind her, hauling the girl's roller bags.

When they reached short-term parking, and Claire stopped in front of Bug, Amanda said, "You got him a paint job, but he still looks old."

"He is old." Claire worked to wrestle two suitcases into Bug's small trunk. She slammed the lid. "You'll have to put the rest on the back seat," she told Amanda.

"You should buy a real car. I picture you in one of those cute mini SUVs," Amanda said.

"Really?" Claire started up Bug.

"Yes, really. This thing is a wreck." She settled back into the seat. "I'm going to get a new car and pick it out myself. Dad always picked my car and handed me the keys. He made the decisions—and I mean all the decisions—but that's done and dusted. It's all about me now."

Distracted by the airport traffic and miffed that Amanda couldn't or wouldn't recognize the differences in their financial status, Claire said, "Amanda let's talk about your father later. Mr. Marsh made you a reservation at the Marriott downtown. Is that okay?"

"Sure, for a couple of nights."

"All right then, we'll head that way unless you need to stop and pick something up."

"I don't need anything."

"Good. You are the firm's top priority. Things are going to be tough for a while, but you're not alone."

"By tough, you mean I'm a suspect, maybe the top suspect because I get all Daddy's money?"

"Mr. Marsh talked to you about what's going to happen, didn't he?" Claire asked.

"No, but what's to talk about? I'm his daughter, and I inherit his money."

Thanks a lot, boss, for paving the way for me.

"Okay, here's what's going to happen. It's routine, just standard operating procedure, but you'll be questioned by the police. The police always look at the family members when a loved one is murdered." Claire glanced over at Amanda. "There's nothing personal about this. Mr. Marsh will be with you every step of the way. In fact, you won't be alone except inside your hotel room. A bodyguard from Eagle Security is waiting for us at the Marriott."

"Wait, let me get this straight. You people think I might have killed Dad, but I need protection? How cuckoo-bananas is that? Ask me, Claire. You're dying to. Ask me if I killed my Dad."

Claire pulled into the circle in front of the Marriott. A bell boy was waiting at the curb. She held up her hand to him letting him know to give them a minute. "Okay, did you kill your Dad?"

Her laughter sounded like the tinkling of little bells. "Nope, didn't do it." She hopped out of the car and waved the bellboy over. "Trunk is in the front of these cars, and there's more baggage in the back seat."

Claire told the valet she didn't want to park Bug, she wasn't staying long. She followed Amanda and the bellboy to the front desk.

Claire checked her in and confirmed the bill would be sent to the firm. She handed Amanda a room key.

"Ms. Tutwiler, Amanda Tutwiler? Over here." A dark-haired, young woman was race-walking across the lobby toward Amanda.

Claire recognized her and stepped in front of Amanda. Kylie Lancaster was a reporter with the *Denver Post*.

"No story here, Kylie," Claire said.

"Oh, c'mon now, Callahan. She's going to talk to someone." Kylie craned her head around Claire. "Ms.

Tutwiler, you remember me? I covered your story a year ago and gave your dad a fair shake in the press."

"Why don't we talk . . ." Amanda said.

Claire cut her off, "If you want a statement, call Marsh &Whitley and talk to Mr. Marsh."

A competent-looking man stepped up. "Ms. Callahan, we got a problem here?" He handed her an Eagle Security business card, and said, "George Ramos."

He turned to Lancaster. "This interview isn't happening." He took Amanda's elbow and steered her toward the elevators.

Lancaster tried to reach around him and hand Amanda her business card, but Claire blocked her.

Lancaster didn't give any ground. She kept tagging along to the elevator. "Call me or I have nothing to lead with but 'Chief Suspect is Dead Man's Daughter.'"

Ramos stopped in front of the elevator, moving Amanda behind him. He turned and faced Lancaster.

The elevator dinged. It was empty, and Claire hurried Amanda inside.

"Call me at the *Post*," Lancaster said. She had to angle her head around Ramos as he stepped into the elevator.

The elevator doors were closing.

"Give me a chance. I want to write your story," Lancaster said before the doors shut.

Ramos introduced himself to Amanda and shook her hand. "Miss Tutwiler, I'll take good care of you."

Claire shook hands with him and slipped him the room key.

Amanda seemed nonplussed by Lancaster's threat. She turned to Claire. "You didn't need to come up to the room with me."

"We need to talk for a moment." Claire was squashing any ideas Amanda had of phoning Lancaster.

Fourteen floors straight up and Ramos stepped out first, checking both ends of the corridor before motioning the women to follow. He went into the room first, leaving them in the entryway.

When he was satisfied the room was safe, Ramos motioned them inside.

"This is ridiculous overkill," Amanda said walking in and tossing her handbag on a chair.

"Ma'am, we don't know that," Ramos said. The other elevator dinged, and the car opened with the bell boy bringing Amanda's bags.

Ramos stopped the bellboy in the doorway. "I'll take it from here."

Claire tipped the bellman, and Ramos brought the bags in and locked the door behind himself.

Amanda pointed to where she wanted the luggage.

Ramos obliged her. "I'll be outside your door. Lock it behind me."

Claire didn't bother to sit in one of the club chairs around the cozy table. "Don't call Kylie Lancaster. Her job is to get people to open up and say things they wouldn't ordinarily say. You're a suspect in a murder case. Nothing good comes of a suspect talking with a journalist. No matter how hard she tries to pretty it up or sweet talk you, she's going to ask a lot of ugly questions about your relationship with your father and your inheritance. The best advice I can give you is, don't talk to anyone but your lawyer or me. Just don't. Let Mr. Marsh speak for you."

"Oh, Claire, you're so over the top. So is all this cloak and dagger crap."

Claire stood her ground, arms crossed, unwavering and not talking.

Amanda's shoulders sagged. "Okay, I won't talk to the woman."

"Good," Claire said, "Now about tomorrow, I'll meet you for breakfast at nine here in the café. Mr. Marsh has a limo service at your disposal. Just call the firm if you want to go anywhere after we eat. Tonight, don't answer the room phone. Only answer your cell if you recognize the number and don't answer your door except to Ramos, Marsh or me. Everything is going to be fine; we just need to be careful."

"Claire, of course, everything is going to be fine. I didn't kill him, and I'm going to be fabulously rich. Stop worrying."

Claire let the comment go unanswered. "Okay then, it's late. Ramos will be right outside. I'll meet you for breakfast at nine."

Once Claire was in the hallway and heading for the elevator, she texted Marsh that Amanda was safely in the hotel.

Downstairs, Claire tipped the valet who was standing by Bug, though there was no reason to think anyone would steal him. She headed home.

She turned on Zuni Street, and her headlights flashed across a gray car parked a couple of houses down from her driveway. She was sure she saw a head duck down when she passed the sedan, but she shook it off. It was three in the morning at the end of a long day. Probably no one had been sitting in a car on a cold night.

The porch light wasn't on, and the duplex was in shadows.

Claire eased her front door open, hoping Kirwin was asleep on the sofa. After dealing with Amanda, she didn't think she had the *oomph* left to tackle Kirwin.

But her luck didn't hold. She tripped over a large

Army-issue duffle bag he'd left inside the front door and went sprawling.

A lamp clicked on.

"Hey Pigeon, sorry about that. The place is so small I didn't have any place to put the bag." Kirwin sat up on the sofa. His thick gray hair was mashed flat on one side. He'd gained weight since she'd seen him, and the extra pounds made him look older and soft. He tilted his head back and finished off the bottle of wine she'd been looking forward to. "Not much booze around here."

"I thought you quit drinking."

He shrugged, and when he grinned, his dimples popped out. He'd disarmed many a mark with that smile and those dimples.

He didn't get up and hug her. It would have been too awkward. She took the chair across from him.

"You look more like your grandmother every time I see you. She was a beauty in her day." His voice was gentle. "You got her brown eyes and copper hair, but you have your mom's nose. I used to tease Ellie something terrible about that nose of hers tilting a tad to the left."

Claire never thought of herself as beautiful. In those awful middle school years of cliques and budding beauty queens, Grandma Callie had told her she was "pretty enough to do."

Claire had no complaints. She'd never been homecoming queen, but she hadn't graduated high school a virgin either.

"Do you have a picture of Eleanor?" Claire asked.

Kirwin pulled the duffle closer and rooted through it. He brought out his wallet. "In here, I only got the one." He passed it over to Claire.

It was a black and white snapshot, a full-body picture, so she couldn't see as much of her face as she wanted. She hadn't seen Eleanor since she'd visited when Claire was about ten years old, and back then, she thought her mother looked like one of the fairy princesses in the stories Callie read to her. "How old is she in the picture?"

"It's way before you were born. Maybe when she was fifteen or sixteen."

Claire took the photo into the kitchen and rooted through the junk drawer for her magnifying glass. When she found it, she saw Eleanor's face was indistinct. She was smiling, and she had the long curly hair Claire remembered, but age and wear—and probably a cheap camera—robbed her of seeing her mother's face clearly.

"I'd like to make a copy for myself. Do you mind?"

"Nah, you go ahead. But don't lose it. It's the only one I got."

"I promise." She returned to the small living room. She was wired and tired, but she had questions for Kirwin. Plenty of them, and he seemed to be in a mood to talk. "I saw you for the first time in decades last year. You told me Eleanor was dead, and then left to go the store for cigarettes and never came back. Didn't you think I had questions about how she died or that I would worry about you?"

"I'm sorry about that. Pigeon, you know I'm no kind of dad. Ellie is your mother. Call her mom."

"Callie was my Mom and Dad all wrapped into one wonderful grandma. Why did you leave me?"

"Sweetheart, we were useless as parents. We slept rough, and Ellie and I begged for food when we didn't steal it."

"Why didn't you at least come visit? Weren't you interested in how I was doing or how Grandma was? Callie was your mother. I didn't even have any way to reach you when she died."

He hung his head. "We were too ashamed, and the longer we stayed away, the easier it was to keep staying away." He reached over and took her hand. "I knew you would be all right with your Grandma. She'd raise you right. My life is no fault on her. She was a good woman."

"What would have happened to me if she died when I was a kid? Did you ever think about me?"

He rested his elbows on his knees and hunched over, not looking at her. "You got to understand, your Mom and me, we were free as birds. We were travelers, didn't think much of anything but ourselves." He squeezed her hand. "I'm sorry, I can't make it up to you, Pigeon."

"Why didn't you tell me goodbye last year? Was that too much for you to do?"

"I couldn't bear the look in your eyes after I told you Ellie was gone. He shook his head. "Ellie and me were always together. Even as kids we knew each other. Ellie was always right by me, and now, she's gone."

"Tell me how she died."

"We were in Chicago and living in the car." He rubbed his hands together. "We was having some bad times."

Claire remembered sleeping alone in the freezing car, huddled under a pile of blankets, scared and waiting for them to come back.

He looked down at his hands. "She got a cold. Nothing really at first, and then she had a fever. I got some aspirin, but it didn't bring the fever down, and she started coughing something bad." He looked up at her searching her face for understanding. "I took her to the hospital. The doc said she had pneumonia. I stood by the bed crying and holding her hand until they told me she was dead, and I had to go. I didn't have nobody to go with me and no place to go." He shrugged. "That's why I showed up here last year."

He lifted his head, tears rolling down his cheeks. "I miss her something terrible."

Claire moved over to the sofa and sat by him, feeling awkward. "Where is she buried?"

"She's in the car."

Claire jumped up. "What?"

"I didn't have the money for a proper burial, so the county cremated her. I keep her with me."

Claire's heart was thumping in her chest. "All right, then. Go get her ashes and bring them inside." Somehow it seemed more respectful to Eleanor to have her in the house than have her spend another night in a freezing car.

Kirwin came back carrying a small cardboard box, softened from handling.

"Put it on the bookshelf," she told him. "We'll get an urn. I don't think the box is going to hold up much longer."

"A proper urn." He smiled. "Ellie would like that." He put the box on the bookshelf and then shrugged off his coat and sat on the sofa.

Claire had so many questions, and she thought Kirwin had enough wine to loosen his tongue. "Where have you been the past year?"

He shifted his eyes to the corner of the room. "Been mostly in Chicago. Moved around some, up around the Lakes".

"Are you in trouble?"

"I made a mistake in Chicago," he mumbled.

"That mistake have anything to do with owing money?"

He shook his head. "I did a favor for guy, an important man, but he don't see it that way."

"What was the favor?"

"You wouldn't understand."

"Try me," Claire said.

Kirwin didn't answer.

"Are the police looking for you?"

"Not that I know of. It's not like that. The cops don't mess with this guy. He's got his hooks in them, too." Kirwin looked up at her. "He don't have any guys in Denver. I'll be all right."

"I hope so because you've brought trouble to my door."

He awkwardly patted her hand. "It's going to be fine, you'll see. I've been here nearly two weeks, and I haven't had a bit of trouble. I got me a job in a warehouse down on Speer. I'll get my own place soon."

"Uh-huh. Where have you been staying?"

"Mostly in the car. Sometimes in the Men's Shelter. You got to wait in line for a bed at the shelter, and sometimes, by the time I got off work, the beds were all filled."

Claire's mind worked through the options. It was a short list. Kick him out or tell him he could stay. *He can stay here* won, but it would come at a price: A promise he'd get professional help.

"What kind of help?" he said suspiciously when she told him.

"For drinking and playing the ponies."

He blew out a long breath. "Okay."

Claire's suspicions went on high alert. That was way too simple. But she was tired, and tomorrow was another day.

"We'll work out the details," she said, "but we have a deal. You can stay if you clean your act up—until you get on your feet." She stood. "I'm going to bed."

She had one more chore to do. Call Truck Tucker.

Truck earned his nickname when he was inside for a couple years and passed the time lifting weights. He came out of prison looking like a jacked-up two-ton truck. The good-hearted state taught him computer skills while he was in prison, and once he was free, he fell in with a hacker associated with Anonymous.

Truck learned a lot, but he wasn't into the mission of Anonymous. He struck out on his own, and if the invoices he sent her were any indication, he made good money.

He could breach any firewall, leave no trace, and keep his mouth shut. He had other skills she used less frequently.

Truck answered on the first ring. "Talk to me," he said.

"I have a new client, Amanda Tutwiler."

"Heard your old client was shot to death," Truck said.

"Yeah, I need everything you can find on her. Call me, and I'll meet you at your office."

Truck agreed. She'd give him a couple of days and then meet him in the back booth in Kwan's Bar on Colfax, a squat two-story building that hadn't changed much since the first Kwan barkeep cooked his booze back in the alley.

Truck lived in an apartment above the bar, and she suspected there was more between the Kwans and Truck than she knew, but she wasn't going to ask.

Claire put on an oversize T-shirt and climbed into bed. She pulled a legal pad and pen off the bedside table.

She drew vertical lines down the yellow sheet, making columns. One she labeled *Who gains by killing Morgan Tutwiler?* And the second, *Who has a grudge to settle?*

Amanda's name looked lonely penciled in the first

column. Those who might harbor a grudge were a more extended list: the Ardens, Devlins, Backstroms, current and former employees—including Hawkins Reynolds— the cook, the yard maintenance crew and the house cleaning service. Basically, anyone he crossed paths with. Tutwiler was no Mr. Rogers.

She fell asleep staring at her notes.

CHAPTER FOUR

Sonja Backstrom sucked in her stomach and yanked her skirt zipper closed. A pudgy roll of flesh bulged over the waistband. Standing before the three-way mirror in her dressing room, she looked over her shoulder at her butt. Good God, her mother's fat ass was staring back at her.

It wasn't fair. She lived off celery sticks and rice cakes, and on top of everything else wrong in her life, now she was turning into her mother.

She snuffled back the tears. They would ruin her make-up and make her eyes puffy, but everyone would think she was grieving. She wiped her nose on a tissue. Hell, she wasn't grieving. She was mad.

Damn you Dave for killing yourself. How could you? Our boy needed you to stick around and help him. He was on his way to turning the business around and printing money. But oh, hell no, you had to take a header off a mountain. I hope you hit every single tree and screamed the whole mile down.

She certainly hadn't held the wake Dave always wanted, him in his casket with his favorite shotgun propped up beside him, the booze flowing, and all the guys singing "Danny Boy." Bullshit. The private graveside service was more than the jackass deserved.

She turned her back on the offending mirror. She'd been a beauty when Dave had swept her off her feet. He would have passed her by if she hadn't been an eyeful.

Dave met her family one time and deemed them hicks. He demanded she cut her ties if she wanted to marry him. She couldn't dump them fast enough. Dave Backstrom was her ticket out of the poorhouse.

Theirs had been a relatively happy marriage until marriage did what marriage does. Peels back the layers spouses hide behind and reveals the things you can't unsee.

Dave's affairs left her feeling adrift and insignificant, but he had given her Luke, her beautiful boy, and she would do anything for her son.

She'd done the hardest thing of all—she'd stayed with Dave when the marriage was dead. She'd rather have her right arm cut off than do anything to impede Luke's chances at success. When her son graduated Wharton, she could hardly contain her excitement. She was a high school dropout from the middle of nowhere, and now was the mother of an Ivy League graduate.

Dave's money provided every opportunity Luke could ever wish for and she'd held up her end of the bargain. She kept her mouth shut.

Luke didn't know a thing about her family. Dave concocted a story of her attending a private college in Montana and their meeting on a ski holiday in Colorado. Luke was a kid. He just took it as fact, and she'd learned to play her part in the lie.

When Dave begin to hit it big with his company, she'd hired a speech coach and a personal fashion assistant, and she'd slipped into Denver society—not for herself, but to pave the way for her boy. No one guessed how far up the ladder she'd climbed.

After a discreet knock on the bedroom door, it opened, and Luke poked his head in.

"Good morning," she said. "Come in."

Luke carried two cups of coffee and the morning papers. Now that Dave was gone, she and Luke took their morning coffee together in her sitting room. The few minutes alone in the mornings with her precious boy were often the best part of her day.

He handed her a coffee and tossed the *Post* on the table between them.

Sonja looked up and saw a troubled face. "What's happened now?"

Luke was blunt as ever. "Morgan Tutwiler was shot to death last night."

Sonja's hand flew to her mouth, and her eyes grew wide. She snatched up the paper and read the first paragraph under the bold headline. Her bottom lip trembled. She looked up at Luke.

"Did you kill him?"

Luke snorted. "I thought you did."

"How could you think that? You didn't answer my question. Did you kill him?" She picked up her coffee. "I can't help you if I don't know the truth."

"No Mother, I didn't shoot him. I wanted to, and you can be sure the cops will be around to talk to us." He paused. "Think about it. I'd say we're tops on their list of suspects." Luke ran his hand through his short hair. "It's not going to help us that when Dad killed himself, the media spouted off he may have driven off Miners Pass because he couldn't take the pressure of his business tanking after the scandal."

Sonja put her coffee on the table, held her spine

ramrod straight off the back of the chair. "What are you going to do?"

"I've called Sam Burnside. He'll be here soon."

"Won't bringing an attorney to the house make us look guilty?"

"We already look guilty. We have a motive, revenge for a very public drubbing, and a huge financial loss."

Sonja twisted her hands in her lap. "If the police investigate us and the reporters make a big deal out of it, every good thing you've done for the business could be wiped out. We could lose it all. We'll be rolling up the rugs and taking the paintings off the walls."

"Settle down. In a bankruptcy, I can hang onto the house. Look, the good news is, we don't gain anything from Tutwiler's death. The cops go after who gets the money, and that's not us. It's Amanda Tutwiler."

"But your father made no bones about hating him, and Tutwiler did destroy our company." Her voice was ratcheting up the scale to hysteria. "They'll think we killed him to get even."

Sonja began crying, her fists clenched at her sides.

"You're all I care about. I don't want anything to happen to you."

"I didn't kill him," Luke said, "so nothing is going to happen to me. Are you taking the medication the doctor prescribed?"

"Yes . . . sometimes."

"Where's the bottle?" Luke asked heading for her bathroom.

"In the medicine cabinet."

Luke returned with the medicine and shook two tablets into her hand, then handed her a glass of water. "You're supposed to take Xanax four times a day every day. Can you do that for me? Both of us need to be on top of our game." All he needed was for her to have another breakdown before he could get her doctor to admit her again.

"I'll take them, it's just that I hate taking medicine."

"We don't have a choice. We have to be our best right now. Here, I'm putting them on your reading table, so you'll see them and remember to take them."

"Okay, I can do that for you."

"It's for us, Mom."

"Right. You and Dave were working a deal with a development company in Boston when he died. Is that deal signed?"

"Done, and it's the largest construction project Millennium has ever taken on."

"I'm proud of you."

Luke puffed up from her praise. "We broke ground last week, and Ingram's son-in-law is coming out to look at the project."

"He's the one you don't like working with, right?"

Luke nodded. "Yeah, Allerton's an idiot on the phone. Ingram keeps him on because he's his son-in-law," Luke looked at his phone to check the time. "Mother, you need to get yourself together. Sam will be here soon. I'll go downstairs and wait for him."

Sonja reached out her hand and took Luke's. "I'd never bet against you. A year ago, no one would have hired Millennium Construction to build a dog house. You're smarter than your Dad was at this age. No matter what we're facing, you'll make it all right. I trust you."

He pecked a kiss on her cheek. "The business is doing better. I'm not letting Tutwiler's murder crap in my breakfast plate." He headed for the doorway.

"Have the cook set up coffee and some pastries in the breakfast area," she said. I'll meet you in a few minutes."

Sonja closed the door behind him, and then sat

down at her dressing table. She stared into the mirror looking at the worry lines dug into the corners of her eyes. Something in Luke's eyes, the way he couldn't look her straight in the face. Her beautiful boy had killed Tutwiler.

She glanced through the article in the *Post*.

Luke said *I didn't shoot him*, but he wouldn't have had to. Construction was a rough and dirty business. Itinerant workers, illegals, workers who were on and off a job site before anyone knew them. Cash changed hands, bribes were paid. And there was always a construction site to bury a body. Why hadn't her smart boy done that? Why did he have Tutwiler killed in his own home and leave the body and a witness? Stupid, stupid, thing to do.

She sucked in a deep breath. Luke wasn't going to prison for killing the most despised man in Denver. The son-of-a-bitch needed killing. Whatever it took, lies, bribes, murder—she'd keep Luke safe.

She touched up her lipstick, shrugged on her suit jacket and felt a tingle of satisfaction. She was the last of the four of them still breathing air. The others were dead, her husband and Lucy Tutwiler, the smug lovers who thought she didn't know about them. Morgan Tutwiler, the man who drove Dave to the grave and tried to run her boy out of business. She turned toward the mirror and preened. She hoped they were all burning in hell.

She was smiling when she walked into the breakfast area.

SAM BURNSIDE ARRIVED ten minutes later.

"Good morning Sonja. You're looking well."

"Thank you, Sam. Please help yourself to some coffee."

Luke waited until Burnside poured cream in his coffee before he spoke. "Mother and I would like you to offer our family's condolences to Amanda."

Burnside cleared his throat and cut his eyes to Sonja, who was staring at Luke.

"We are establishing a scholarship at Colorado State University as a memorial to Amanda's father," Luke continued.

"I'm a bit surprised in light of all that has happened between the families," Burnside said, "but it's a gracious thing for you to do. Certainly, I can help you set up the endowment, and I'll draft a letter of condolences for you to approve."

It was a strategic move, and the wily old lawyer knew it.

"Moving onto other business," Luke said, "I want you to represent Mother and me. I expect the police will be around to question us."

"Of course." Sam said. "I think that is the wisest course of action. The police may call to set an appointment or just show up at your door. Either way, don't speak to them unless I'm present. I think the questioning will be quite rigorous. I expect they'll hammer you about Dave nearly losing his business while Tutwiler's net worth flourished. They'll bring up the death of the young mother on the bridge, the civil suits, the millions of dollars in contracts Millennium lost over the bridge collapse."

Luke interrupted, irritated. "We lived through it. We know what happened."

"Of course, you did," Sam said, "I was there too. The police will force you to relive it. They'll take you back through the last year step by step, hoping the emotional stress has you telling them something they can use against you."

"It's hard to look like we snapped and killed him under emotional duress when we're setting up a memorial fund for him," Sonja said.

"That helps," Sam agreed, "but it doesn't indemnify you. Remember, for an interview, you have a right to a lawyer. Don't talk to the police without me at your side. And call me if they show up with a warrant to search the house."

"Are you expecting them to come with a warrant?" Luke asked.

"No, not really, but if they do, just call me, and I'll take care of everything. We have to be prepared for every eventuality." He paused. "One more thing. No talking to the media. Don't even say, 'No comment.' The talking heads will opine on the air as to the meaning of why you won't comment. Don't discuss Amanda, Tutwiler's death, or any issues with the Tutwiler family with anyone. Not even that you set up a memorial fund. That includes friends and family members. The police will interview them, too."

Luke and Sonja agreed.

"Just so we're all clear on this, Mom and I have nothing to gain from Tutwiler's death," Luke reminded Sam.

"And that is exactly the point we'll make over and over. Both of you should keep to your usual routines. You've done nothing wrong. Luke, you have a business to run and Sonja, you have your charity work."

Sonja stood. "Thank you, Sam. I have a meeting with the Friends of the Library to discuss a fundraiser. Luke, I have some things I want to talk with you about later in the day."

Sam stood and grabbed his coat off a chair. "Good

place for you to be seen, Sonja. Exactly what you should be doing. I'll be at the office. If you need me, I'll drop everything and come."

Sonja left, and Luke saw Sam Burnside to the door, before going into the study and shutting the door behind him. The staff and his mother were instructed not to bother him when the door was closed.

He poured a healthy slug of Jameson in a Baccarat Crystal glass and put his feet up on his Dad's desk. His desk now.

He'd been amped when he hired a killer to murder Tutwiler. Then the morning *Post* arrived, and his confidence took a nosedive. He'd read the story twice. The newspaper story didn't jive with what he'd paid for. Tutwiler's body was supposed to never be found, and there certainly wasn't supposed to be a witness left to blab about it. For $50K, it was a damn crappy job leaving a witness alive and the body lying on the guy's living room floor.

Good God, what happened?

All morning, Luke had been jumping at the sound of every car passing the house, and his heart had nearly leapt from his throat when the doorbell rang—even though he'd been expecting Sam Burnside.

He was a detail man and he'd made careful plans to have Tutwiler killed. He confided in a friend of a friend that he needed someone to make a problem go away— and it couldn't be traced back to him. The guy asked for Luke's cell number and told him he'd be hearing from someone, and it wouldn't be him. He'd been emphatic his involvement with Luke's problem was over.

A couple of days later, Luke got a text from a blocked number, telling him to buy a burner phone and text his new burner number to the number provided.

He bought the phone and sent the text. A week

passed before he received detailed instructions, and he did exactly as he was asked.

He delivered $50,000 to a GPS point on the old Ute Trail in Rocky Mountain National Park. High above the tree line, where the entire trail was wide open to the sky, he wedged the bag of money into a fissure in a rock.

It was the perfect location for the drop, no phone service, no way to trace him up there, and nothing for a camera to be attached to. Up on the tundra, nothing grew higher than the lichen covering the rocks.

There were cameras on the ranger stations at the entrance to the park. His visitor pass was scanned, and the same ranger was manning the booth when he drove out. He had nothing to worry about. He was a regular visitor and he'd made a point of telling his office staff he was taking the afternoon off.

He received one more directive after the drop.

Destroy the burner phone.

With the burner gone, he had no way of reaching the people he hired. He could kick himself in the pants for not writing down the burner's number. But they probably had destroyed the phone they used. They sure as hell knew how to contact him. They had his personal cell number.

Damn, he was left hanging in the wind. He poured another belt of whiskey.

What was it the storied Wharton School of Business had taught him?

To expose and challenge his assumptions.

He assumed the guy he hired murdered Tutwiler.

But the more he thought about it, the more he believed someone else beat him to the punch and killed Tutwiler before his guy had a chance to.

There sure as hell was no shortage of people who would like to kill him.

The guy he hired was probably laughing his ass off with his 50k in his pocket, and Luke couldn't touch him.

He poured more whiskey in his coffee and talked himself off the ledge.

You got this. No one could prove he hired a hit but the guy who took the contract, and he wasn't going to talk. There was no evidence tying him to Tutwiler's death. If someone wanted to look at the books, he'd move cash from his home safe to the office safe and there would be no trace of the 50K he'd taken out of the company.

At least Tutwiler was dead.

CHAPTER FIVE

Claire left Bug with the Marriott valet and walked to the café to meet Amanda for breakfast.

Amanda was sipping coffee at a table by the windows overlooking the pool. Looking just as fashionable as the night before in skinny jeans tucked into the same suede boots and a slouchy, navy blue cowl-neck sweater.

Claire was in black tailored slacks, a silk shirt—because she was meeting a client—and low-heeled black shoes that were more comfortable than fashionable.

"Good morning," Claire said as she pulled out a chair.

"Good morning to you too. I'm ready to order. I'm having coffee and dry toast. You?"

"I need a minute with the menu," Claire said.

A waitress approached and asked if Claire wanted coffee.

"We're ready," Amanda said and ordered her breakfast.

Claire looked up from the menu she'd had no time

to read. "Uh, sure, I'd like coffee and an egg white omelet with wheat toast."

When the waitress left Claire asked, "Did you get some sleep?"

"Oh, cut the crap, Claire. I'm not a little girl. No one cares whether I slept well or not. This is all business. You wouldn't be here if you didn't work for Charles Marsh. Dad's dead and Marsh just sees me as a buttload of billable hours."

"I'm sorry you feel that way. I lost my grandmother and I know how it hurts to miss someone. I do work for Mr. Marsh, but I also care about you."

Amanda did a long sigh. "I didn't mean to bite your head off. I just hate what's going to happen."

"What do you think is going to happen?" Claire asked.

"Everyone is going to be all solemn and offer me their sympathy. I don't need their sympathy. I didn't love him. I was dying for his attention when I was a kid. Then I gave up. He was never going to notice me. All that yearning turned to loathing. He held the purse strings, and I had to dance to his tune." She made jazz hands. "Look at me now. I'm emancipated."

"Don't say that to anyone else but your lawyer or a counselor."

Amanda shrugged. "People probably already know. It's an old story. Poor little rich girl hates her Daddy." She paused, looking out the window. Then her face lit up. "Hey, let's have some fun. Let's go shopping after breakfast."

Claire shook her head. "I'm sorry, but I have to work."

"You'd be working taking me around. I know Mr. Marsh is making you act like my friend. Just like you did when Dad was your client. Wait, I'm the client now, right?"

"Yes, you're the client, but I'm not acting. I am your friend. I can't go shopping because I have several meetings, including one with Mr. Marsh." A white lie. She could hardly tell Amanda she was attending her father's autopsy this morning. "You have a busy day yourself, a meeting with your attorney and . . ."

"Getting grilled by the cops," Amanda finished. "Okay, tonight. Maybe dinner and drinks, too?"

"That would be great. I'll stay in touch if I'm going to be late."

"Good, I'll set up an appointment to get your hair done at The Salon at Cherry Creek. I can get in some shopping while you're with the stylist." Amanda sat back smiling.

"I don't need a haircut," Claire said.

"You need a *hairstyle*. They'll do a fabulous job. That messy bun does nothing for you."

The waitress brought the food, saving Claire from responding to the hair critique. The messy bun comment put a damper on her mood, and the breakfast conversation broke down. They ate in silence.

Claire was no psychologist, but even she saw Amanda could use the help of the therapist she'd been seeing before she moved to Boston. Amanda was one angry chick.

Claire ate half the omelet and made a show of checking the time. "I have to get moving if I'm going to make my meeting. Jenny will be in touch with you to talk about the limo service and your meeting with Mr. Marsh this afternoon."

"No problem. I'll shop the boutiques in the hotel this morning."

Claire said her goodbyes, paid for breakfast and left a generous tip.

The valet brought Bug around and commented that his grandfather had driven a Beetle just like Bug. Some folks appreciated her car more than Amanda, who wanted to banish him to the junk heap.

Traffic was heavy, and the drive took longer than usual. Idling at yet another red light, Claire thought how uncomfortable Kirwin looked this morning scrunched up on her short sofa, his legs and feet hanging off the end.

At the next red light, she scrolled through her contacts and found the number of the department store where she had purchased her mattress. She explained to the salesman—twice—she didn't want the box springs, charged a twin-size mattress to her card, and arranged the delivery.

Then she called Kirwin to tell him to be home and let them in. Of course, he didn't answer. She left him a message stressing the importance of him going directly home after work.

If he wasn't there, would porch pirates steal a mattress?

Worse, was she enabling Kirwin by buying him a bed?

She pulled around to the back of the three-story law office and parked in the garage.

A set of carved double doors led from the parking garage to the firm. Reception and Records were located on the first floor. The associates toiled in their cubicles on the second floor, competing for the coveted status of junior law partner in the firm. She always thought the same thing when she rode past their floor: There were many more associates than available junior partnerships, and many would be shown the door at the end of five years of drudgery.

The partners had offices on the third floor, where she had a tiny office with a window giving her a glorious view of the Rockies.

The elevator opened into a large open space lined on two sides with private offices and conference rooms. The west wall was floor-to-ceiling glass with a view of downtown and a backdrop of the Rockies. The dove gray walls, luxurious leather furniture, and oil paintings were all selected to soothe the anxieties of the big money clients.

Claire closeted herself in her office to organize her thoughts before reporting to Marsh.

Her desk phone rang—Jenny telling her Marsh was ready to meet.

Claire grabbed a pen and legal pad, then headed down the hall to rap on the open door to Marsh's office.

He looked up from a mountain of paperwork. "Come in." He gestured to a chair in front of his desk. "First, tell me how Amanda is."

Claire chose her words carefully. "I think she's frightened, but it comes across as anger."

"Do you think we should try to get her see the therapist she was seeing during the trial?" What was that woman's name?" Marsh asked.

"I'll track it down. Yeah, Amanda needs help. She's all over the place, thrilled to go shopping and talking about how happy she is her dad's dead. She's going to be a handful. Kylie Lancaster was lying in waiting at the Marriott. I hustled Amanda into the elevator before she could say anything and read her the riot act about talking to the press, but I don't think she sees giving an interview as a problem. Lancaster will come after her again, and I may not be there to run her off."

Marsh scraped his hand from his mouth down to his Adam's apple, bunching the loose skin of his neck at his shirt collar. "Lord what a mess. I'll caution her about the press. Do you think Amanda could have killed her father?"

"It's possible she hired someone to murder him."

He took his glasses off and pinched the bridge of his nose. "Did she tell you she and her Dad hadn't talked to each other in a year? That I was the go-between?"

Claire shook her head.

Marsh put his glasses back on. "Damn, the hits just keep coming. We have to keep the Tutwiler legal business in the firm. I know that sounds selfish and I do care about the girl. I've known her most of her life and I feel sorry for her. Neither of her parents gave her a lick of attention." He paused, tapping a finger on the desk, then shrugged. "Yeah, I know. Who am I to criticize? I wasn't Daddy-of-the-year material myself."

Claire looked at him as passively as possible. She knew his story. Too many late nights and weekends in the office. Next thing Marsh knew, his girls were grown and gone.

Marsh looked tired and on edge. "Does your detective friend think she's in any danger?"

"Rafe thinks she needs to be careful."

"That's detective-speak for she might get killed," Marsh said. "How bad is Hawkins's wound?"

"It looked to me like a shoulder wound. He was conscious and talking. It was Hawkins who made the 911 call."

"I always liked him. What evidence do the police have?"

"Two eyewitnesses, fingerprints, and a set of footprints," Claire said, then paused and continued,

"You know there's no shortage of people who wanted him dead."

Marsh nodded. "He was no joy to be around. Did they get a match on the fingerprints?"

Claire shook her head. "No match to any database."

"Surely there's a good description of the killer. He passed by the gate guard, and Hawkins let him in the house," Marsh said.

"No, not really. The gate guard and Hawkins described him as a young white guy with dark hair."

"That's worthless." Marsh threw out his hands. "I can't believe Hawkins couldn't do better than that. He's had military training, and the guy was right there in the hallway with him. Hawkins looked him in the eye before he got shot. You always remember the guy who shot you."

Claire nodded her head. "I agree, but Hawkins claims he didn't recognize him, and he would know anyone who had prior dealings with Tutwiler. That doesn't mean anyone is off the hook. Anyone of them could have hired a hitman."

"You don't suspect Hawkins, do you? He's not a killer," Marsh said. "He's been Tutwiler's majordomo for twenty years. He had Tutwiler's back during the divorce, and when Tutwiler and Backstrom were receiving death threats about the bridge collapse. He's loyal to the bone."

Claire nodded. "Exactly how much money does Hawkins get?"

"Two years' salary," Marsh said, "and that's not enough to kill for. Hawkins lives above the garage rent free. No financial reason to kill his boss." Marsh leaned back in his chair and steepled his fingers. "Is that what the cops think? That Hawkins killed Tutwiler?"

"I don't know what Rafe thinks. I know Hawkins opened the door to a killer."

"How does Hawkins explain his actions?"

"I'll know after I talk to Rafe. He's at the hospital interviewing him."

"I want to hear what he says." Marsh narrowed his eyes. "Are you taking good care of Amanda?"

"We had breakfast this morning, and we're going shopping tonight."

"Good, I knew you'd take her in hand," Marsh said. He pushed his chair back from his desk indicating the meeting was over. "I want you here at two for our meeting with Amanda. Our joint meeting will be short. I have to prepare her for her police interview."

***

SHE PULLED in next to Rafe's Ford Escape at the county medical examiner's office, a two-story nondescript, beige building, probably built during Denver's boom in the seventies.

The building was nothing to look at from the street, but inside, it had state-of-the-art autopsy suites, a morgue, and well-equipped toxicology and histology labs. The autopsy suites and staff offices were on the first floor. The labs occupied the second floor.

She opened the front door, and even in the vestibule, the smell of disinfectant mingled with air freshener.

Once past the guard at the front desk, she went to a small anteroom and put on protective clothing. Suited up, she walked into the autopsy suite.

Rafe was already standing at the stainless-steel table. She took up a position by him.

Iverson and Loretta, his longtime assistant, were over by the body coolers.

Iverson glanced up. "Good, you're both here. Let's get this started."

Iverson helped his assistant move the body onto the table.

Loretta placed a rubber block under Tutwiler's torso arching his chest and abdomen for easier access to Iverson's scalpel. Then, she yanked on the body's ankles, straightening his lower torso.

She flipped on the high-intensity lights over the body. "You need anything else?" she asked Iverson.

He shook his head and slipped on his splash shield. Then, he lowered the overhead microphone into place, turned it on and began his dictation.

"Both X-Ray and CT imaging show two bullets lodged in the left side of the chest. Minimal stippling and powder residue were found at the wound sites."

He turned the microphone off and said to Rafe: "Look at the slide mounted under the microscope."

Rafe turned around and looked through the microscope on a work counter behind them. He looked up at Claire and raised his eyebrows. "See what you think."

"Looks like a brown hair," Claire said.

"It's not," Iverson said. "It's cellulose from the oil filter the killer used as a silencer. The brown coloring is motor oil. I picked it out of both his wounds."

"Smart guy. Soaked the oil filter to suppress the gunshot more," Rafe said.

"Exactly," Iverson said. "Get your forensic team to take fibers from the rug he died on. They should find the same fibers."

Claire leaned in close to Rafe and whispered, "Hawkins should have noticed a honking big oil filter screwed on the barrel."

Rafe mouthed the word *Later*.

Iverson picked up a scalpel and made a Y incision, the two arms of the Y running from the shoulder joints to mid-chest, the stem down to the pubic area. With a pair of shears, he snapped through the cartilage freeing the rib cage, then lifted it off and set it aside.

Iverson pointed with a gloved finger. "You can see the damage to the lower left side of the heart. The left anterior descending artery was severed by a bullet, ceasing the flow of blood to the front and bottom of the left ventricle and the front of the septum. That's what killed him."

He probed the muscle layer behind the heart. A few quick cuts with a scalpel, and he pulled out the bullet.

"Nine-millimeter hollow point." He held it up for them to see. "The nose is peeled back like a banana." He adjusted the light over the chest cavity and pointed into the dissected area. "And there's the flat burst in the tissues when the bullet mushroomed."

With the cause of death officially established, Rafe was reaching to pull off his gown. "Thanks, Irv."

Rafe and Claire stuffed their gowns and shoe covers in the trash on the way out of the autopsy suite.

"Got time for a quick lunch?" Rafe said once they were in the hallway. "There's a Mongolian diner around the corner with a buffet lunch."

"Are you going to tell me what Hawkins had to say at the hospital?"

"Yeah, c'mon. We can walk it faster than driving around looking for a place to park."

Claire was no shorty at five-six, but Rafe was a good head taller. She had to race-walk to keep up with him.

The lunch crowd was gone, and the diner was nearly empty. They had their pick of booths, and Rafe chose one in the back facing the front door. A waitress took their drink orders and told them to help themselves to the buffet.

A couple of the pans were already scraped empty. Claire helped herself to a chicken dish and took the last of the steamed rice. She left Rafe at the buffet, trying to add more food to his loaded plate. He tackled the buffet like a single guy.

As soon as he sat down, she said, "Tell me Hawkins's version of what happened."

He swallowed and pointed his fork at her. "Shortly after five, Tutwiler had dinner in his office. Hawkins and the cook ate in the kitchen and then Hawkins helped the cook clean up. She had plans to see a movie with a friend and left by five-thirty. He was still tidying up the kitchen when the doorbell rang."

"Why was Tutwiler in his bathrobe so early?" Claire asked.

Rafe dabbed at his mouth. "Tutwiler played racquetball at his club from three to four, then Hawkins drove him home. He showered and put the robe on as soon as he got home."

"Right." Claire pointed at Rafe. "They had all eaten dinner. Tutwiler's in his office in his bathrobe. They weren't expecting anybody. Why would his majordomo, who stood by his side all last year when the death threats were flying, open the door to a stranger?"

"I can only tell you what he told me," Rafe said. "Hawkins says he opened the door to tell the guy he was at the wrong house and point him in the right direction. Hawkins claims pizza delivery men are a dime a dozen in the neighborhood, and Huber confirmed that. Hawkins feels like shit for getting his boss killed."

Claire toyed with her food. "With what went down last year, Hawkins would know better than to open the door to someone he wasn't expecting, even though he never served in the military."

Rafe looked up at her, surprised.

"I checked, no record of service for a Hawkins Reynolds."

"So, he lied about serving." Rafe shrugged. "Maybe he thought it would impress Tutwiler enough to hire him. He's worked for the guy two decades. Must have done something right along the way. Maybe he had a momentary lapse in judgment and opened the door."

Claire cocked her head. "I'm not sure I buy it. How bad is his wound?"

"The doc says his shoulder should heal without any surgery. They patched him up and started an IV. Guess who was kissing him when I arrived? Beverly Bryant," he said before Claire could guess. "She excused herself and left when she saw me."

"What do you make of that?" Claire asked.

Rafe shrugged. "They're about the same age, both single. Could be Hawkins is just getting it on with the neighbor."

"Two years of his salary," Claire said, "is not enough to keep Bryant in the style she's accustomed to."

"Two years of his salary isn't going to compensate for his guilt over opening the door," Rafe pointed out. "Plus, he just lost his job."

"I don't know that he'll lose his job," Claire said. "Amanda has always been fond of him. I bet she keeps him on."

"We'll have to see how that plays out." Rafe shoved his empty plate away from him. "Hawkins says the killer spoke to him on the way out of the house. 'The old man's dead'—which doesn't sound like it was worth the breath it took to say it."

"What?" Claire said, surprised. "Hawkins never said that last night. Is he making it up?"

Rafe threw out both hands. "I don't think so, but what the hell good is the statement anyway? You pointed out Hawkins has no military experience. He's a civilian, and he'd been shot and was practically in shock. It's a throw-away comment."

"It's terribly convenient," Claire said. "'The old man's dead.' Oh, come on Rafe. Totally covers Hawkins's butt for not trying to help Tutwiler."

"He's embarrassed about not rendering aid."

"Oh, goody, he's embarrassed. That makes it so much better. Rafe, I can't believe you think this is what happened."

"I didn't say I believed him. I'm telling you what he told me. He also told me this morning that a blue thing was stuck on the end of the gun."

"That's why you weren't surprised at the autopsy. You already knew."

"I suspected. Witnesses usually give more detail in the second interview."

"Okay, what brand of oil filters are blue?"

"TopCan. It's cheap and sold everywhere."

"That won't help us," Claire said. "Anymore revelations from Hawkins?"

"Yeah, he said the pizza uniform looked about two sizes too small on the killer."

"I hate to think where the guy is who owns the uniform."

"He'll turn up." Rafe pushed his plate aside and said, "We vetted the lawn crew and the maid service. They don't send the same employees each time they work at the house. Both companies have a roster of contract workers and assign crews each morning. We ran every employee of both companies. No red flags.

The cook's worked for Tutwiler over a decade. Nothing suspicious about her, not even a speeding ticket."

"Well, someone sure was mad enough to screw a homemade silencer on the end of his gun, drive over, and shoot him."

"Let's start with the short list," Rafe said. "Who is the person who gains? His daughter. What do you think of her now that you've seen her?"

"She's very fashionable." Claire checked the time. "I have a client meeting with her and Marsh in about half an hour, so I'm out of here." Claire wasn't giving away any details about a client under suspicion for murder.

Rafe didn't give her any push back.

They split the bill and walked to their cars.

CHAPTER SIX

Claire joined Marsh in the conference room shortly before their meeting with Amanda. A coffee service, a platter of cookies, and a pitcher of lemon water were on the table. "Wow," Claire said. "From the Eighteenth Street Bakery. Love their cookies."

"Help yourself, I can't eat them," Marsh said. "Was the autopsy routine?"

Claire decided cookies didn't sound so tasty if she was going to talk about an autopsy. Instead, she poured herself some lemon water. "There were no surprises. One of the bullets nicked an artery, and he died quickly."

"Good, maybe Amanda will take comfort in knowing he didn't suffer." He poured himself a cup of coffee. "Have you talked with Rafe?"

Claire nodded.

"Does he have any evidence implicating Amanda?" Marsh asked.

"No, and I don't either, but it's early in the investigation."

"Amanda's innocent. Prove that up. The kid holds

the key to my financial future." Marsh leaned in a little closer to Claire. "But I need you to cover my ass. I don't know a damn thing about what she's been up to in Boston in the last year. Find out."

"I'll take care of it," Claire said. Good to have the boss's approval to snoop on the client, since Truck was already working on it.

"And take a hard look at the Backstroms, and the Arden and Devlin families," Marsh added. "They got hurt the worst last year."

Jenny knocked on the door, then stuck her head in. "Amanda's driver texted, and he's just parked in our garage."

"Thanks, Jenny. Please go meet Amanda and walk her up."

Jenny left, and Marsh looked at Claire. "Keep her happy. Got it?"

"Absolutely."

Jenny returned with Amanda. This morning, Amanda was dressed like a young professional, narrow leg black wool pants topped by a shawl-collared, slightly oversized chalk stripe jacket. Underneath the jacket, she wore a black silk shell.

Amanda's eyes darted around the room, finally settling on Claire.

"Good morning," Claire said. Once again, she felt underdressed. She envied Amanda's sense of style and her clothes.

Amanda pulled out a chair and sat down. "I like that blouse. The color is perfect for you." She turned her attention to Marsh. "Nice to see you. It's been a long time."

Marsh got up and walked around the table and hugged her. "Yes, too long. Good to have you back in Denver." Marsh sat down and glanced at his papers.

"I'm sorry we have to meet under these circumstances. I'll try to make it brief. We have some business we have to attend to, but first I want to answer any questions you might have."

"I have some instructions for you, and of course, I want you to help with the cops this afternoon."

Marsh kept a poker face. "As you wish. We'll need a client agreement signed for confidentiality reasons before I can go to work for you. We can do that now if you are agreeable."

"Whatever." She waved her hand. "I'll sign."

Marsh picked up the phone and punched in Jenny's extension. He asked her to bring a client agreement form.

While they waited, Amanda asked: "So besides me, who else is a suspect in Dad's murder?"

"Detective Brewster would be the best person to answer that question." Marsh steered the conversation to business. "The firm is proud to have represented your family for decades, and we look forward to taking care of you. I know this is a very difficult time, but this firm is here to guide you through the decisions you'll need to make in regard to your father's passing."

There was a knock on the door, and Jenny walked in, handing Marsh some papers.

He thanked her and put his half-glasses on, glancing through them before flipping to the last page and signing. He handed them to Amanda. "This is a standard agreement between a law firm and a client. Take your time and read it before signing." He handed it to her.

Amanda flipped to the back page, scribbled her name across the bottom, and handed it back to Marsh. "I don't know the contents of my father's will."

"Your father didn't change his will," Marsh said.

"He loved you very much. Other than small bequests to Hawkins and the cook, you inherit everything including all his business interests. The house must be released by the police, and of course, the estate must pass through probate. Then it is all yours to do with as you please."

"So, when can I move into the house?"

"Is the hotel unsatisfactory? The firm will put you up wherever you want," Marsh said.

"No, if the house is mine, I want to live in it."

Claire leaned forward. "I'll talk to Detective Brewster and see when the house will be released. But there is still the probate process to consider. These things take some time to work through."

Amanda's face was unbending. "As soon as possible, I'd like to walk through the house. Only Hawkins or I would know if something has been stolen."

"I'll let Detective Brewster know you would like to do that," Claire said.

"And I want all of Hawkins' hospital bills paid from the estate," Amanda said.

"Very generous of you. I'll take care of it," Marsh said. "Would you like us to help you make arrangements for your father's funeral?"

"There won't be a funeral."

Marsh was gentle and fatherly. "I understand you want privacy. We can arrange a private graveside service if you like."

"I don't want any service."

"I see. Your Dad purchased two burial plots when your mom passed, I believe he wanted to be buried beside her."

"He's not going to be. Bury him in another cemetery and if you can, bury him upside down with his feet sticking out."

Remarkably, Marsh didn't react. "I understand how difficult and sudden the tragedy is for you."

"I'm not traumatized. Why doesn't anyone understand? He was a pain in the ass, and he's dead. I don't want to talk about him anymore."

"As you wish," Marsh said. "Perhaps, you have other business you wish to discuss?"

"Yes, as soon as the estate clears probate, I want to sell all of the businesses that are a part of Tutwiler Industries, and bank the money," she said.

Marsh lost his poker face, and his mouth gaped open. He dropped his head, and when he looked up, he was composed. "I suggest we hire a top-notch adviser from the estate's assets to guide you in the best way to secure income from the wealth you've inherited."

Amanda smiled. "Thank you for the offer. I have a business plan in place."

"I see," Marsh said. "So, you have someone in Boston who is advising you? The firm will be happy to work with him or her."

She leaned forward. "This money management business is not rocket science. No one is more interested in my money than I am, and no one cares more about my future than I do. I got this covered."

Marsh said, "I would be derelict in my duties if I didn't advise you to wait six months before you did anything, and at the end of six months, I'll still advise you to hire a professional money manager."

"Good, you're not a derelict and you did your due diligence. Now, find me a broker for the businesses. I have no intention of running a bunch of companies my father founded."

Claire noticed Amanda was trembling.

Rage or grief? Claire couldn't tell, but she had been right. Amanda was a handful.

"I don't even want to be saddled with the Tutwiler name," Amanda said. "I'm thinking of changing my name to my mother's maiden name."

"Amanda, you don't have to do anything today," Marsh said. "I'd advise you to wait before you make any major decisions. Is there someone you'd like to call to stay with you, or someone you would like to talk with? Perhaps the therapist you were seeing before you moved to Boston?"

Amanda took a long breath in through her nose before exhaling. "Claire's fine. I don't believe in all that psychology bullcrap about vomiting your guts out to some counselor to make yourself feel better."

Claire's heart sank to her toes.

Nooo. Her job was to work the case, not be her psychologist, her hand-holder, her human tissue. But she knew what Marsh would say: *Take her in hand.*

Amanda put up a hand as though to ward off further talk from Marsh. "I want you to tell me what to say to the cops."

"It's nothing to worry about. I'll be acting as your representative," Marsh said. "Very normal under the circumstances, but don't speak to the police without me present."

"You didn't answer my question," Amanda said. "Go on, ask me. You want to know if I killed him. That's why you didn't say tell the truth."

Marsh's face hardened. "I won't ask you if you killed him and I strongly counsel you not to offer me an answer. If you tell me you killed your father, I can't tell the jury you're innocent. I can't lie in court, nor can I allow you to take the stand and perjure yourself by offering an alibi that I know is false."

Amanda turned to look at Claire. "Wow, Claire— he's as uptight as you are."

Claire tried to control her impatience. "Amanda, the death penalty was reinstated in Colorado in 1974 with over sixty percent of the citizens voting in favor of it. That's the kind of people who will be sitting on the jury. Whoever killed your father could be facing a death sentence. If that's not something to be uptight about, tell me what is. If you need a grief counselor or some time alone, we have all kinds of resources at our fingertips. Just say the word. Amanda, we *are* your team."

The young woman flicked her hand. "Whatever." But she did look slightly abashed. "What kind of questions are the cops going to ask me?"

"Simple questions." Marsh smiled. "Where you were during the time of his death, who you might have been with during that time."

"Oh, you mean who might be my alibi?" she asked.

"Yes," Marsh said, "where were you that night?"

"In class. I had Western Civilization with Professor Kotterna from five to eight the night he was killed."

"Good answer," Marsh said. "Expect them to follow up with who was in the class, and they will question your friends at school and your neighbors. Keep your answers short. Don't get involved in long stories about what you think, or what your friends said. They'll be recording this, both audio and video, and may call a police psychologist in to look at the recording. Keep your answers simple."

"Is there anything in your financial records that might raise a red flag?" Claire asked.

"You mean did I write a check to a hit man?" Amanda asked. Then she turned to Marsh. "You transfer money from my trust into my account every month, and by the way, I'm broke before the month ends. You can see my financial records online."

Marsh nodded. "Good, honest answer. Tell it to

them just like you told me. Now, I'll ask you not to respond to a question if I think it's not in your best interest. The question we need to think about is how you will answer when they ask you about your relationship with your father."

Amanda crossed her legs and leaned back. "Just tell me what to say."

"The truth. You were both still grieving the loss of your mother. You had your differences during some difficult times, but you were family."

"Yeah, sure, I can say that," Amanda said, "but the household staff, like Hawkins, knows what was really going on."

"Your job is to concentrate on your answers. Don't think about what anyone else might say. The less detail you provide, the less there is for the police—or potentially the District Attorney—to pick apart. Don't embellish. Just stick to the facts, you lost your mother, and then your father had a business crisis, and these put a great strain on both of you. The police will ask you the same questions over and over. Give the same answer each time. That's why you keep them short and true."

Amanda nodded her head. "What if they ask me if I killed him?"

"That's when I'll step in and tell you not to answer. You can't be asked to incriminate yourself."

"And if they ask me if I know who killed him, then what?"

"I'll tell you not to answer. You're going to do fine."

"This will all be over soon, and you can return to school in Boston," Claire said.

Marsh added, "Yes, you'll need to finish your education. I told my girls many times how important it is for a woman to be educated."

Amanda smiled. "Who says I'm going back to

Boston? I'm staying in Denver." She abruptly stood. "If you'll excuse me, I need to use the restroom." She headed for the conference room door but paused in the doorway and looked over her shoulder at them. "You two feel free to talk about me while I'm gone." She closed the door behind her.

Marsh waited a beat after the door shut. Then he leaned closer to Claire and whispered, "We've got our work cut out for us."

"That we do."

"Someone is influencing her. Someone she met in Boston," Marsh said. "On her own, she would have never come up with the idea of selling the businesses. She would just want to know how much money she would get every month. And I've never heard her utter the words 'business plan', much less have a plan." He paused. "Make yourself available for her to talk to. She'll start feeling closer to you, and it'll be harder for her to pull away from the firm. Find out who the outside influence is. Then I'll neutralize him or her."

He checked his Rolex for the time.

"I'm going to spend the next twenty minutes running her through questions and letting her practice her answers. I'll make your apologies to her."

CLAIRE HEADED to her office to do background on the Backstroms. Marsh had mentioned them twice, and she'd have a report ready the next time he brought their name up.

The Backstroms owned Millennium Construction and had partnered with Tutwiler's steel company to build a new bridge over the Platte River. Everything that could go wrong did—including a wrongful death suit and a criminal indictment. Fines were paid, the civil suits were settled out of court and an undisclosed plea deal closed the criminal case.

Millennium Construction took a heavier hit than Tutwiler because Tutwiler was diversified. He'd sold the steel company, but Tutwiler kept the brew pubs, a bank, and a logging company, all of which kept him rolling in money.

The Backstroms owned only the construction company, and their business dried up. Who would hire a guy whose bridge fell in the river?

Claire turned to the Internet and searched for gold in the databases the law firm subscribed to.

Dave Backstrom's widow, Sonja, was fifty-one, owned a home on Dry Creek Road valued at nearly a million dollars, and had no arrest record. She'd married David Backstrom when she was 19, and he was 31. Their only child, Lucas David Backstrom, was 27.

Luke attended the Wharton School of Business and cut his teeth with a business bank in Philadelphia before returning to Denver and buying a condominium near his parent's home. Luke had a ringside seat for the trial, the subsequent decline of the family business, and his father's suicide. He was now the sole owner and operator of Millennium Construction.

Claire bet the company was still struggling to regain its reputation.

Claire checked the company's website. They had two projects under construction, a condominium project in Capitol Hill, and The Market on Main in downtown.

On Millennium's home page, *The Market on Main* was a hotlink to a real estate developer's page. Claire clicked the link to the Ingram and Mellor home page. I&M touted themselves as the premier commercial real estate development company on the East Coast.

If the Backstroms had a contract with a major player back east, why would Dave Backstrom kill himself?

Something she should ask Luke Backstrom.

She pulled up the building permits for the Market on Main. On a sizable tract of prime real estate in downtown, Millennium was building a shopping area that would also house boutiques, bars, and eateries, as well as high-end living spaces in twin towers.

It appeared Luke was turning the business around.

Luke didn't post often on Facebook. His last post was of him standing by a bright red Porsche 911 in a picture that looked like it had been taken at the dealership. He was tall and blond, resting one hand on the hood of the Porsche.

Maybe the car was a lease and for show to impress clients. She didn't know where he would have gotten the money for the car. The real money wouldn't roll in until the projects were finished.

One thing was sure, after being raked over the coals by Tutwiler, Luke and his mom had plenty to be angry about.

She grabbed her bag and phone and headed down to the garage.

She'd surprise Luke with his guard down and control the conversation until he gathered his wits.

The Marsh and Whitley law firm was in south central Denver, and the construction company was in a high rise in central downtown. Claire used the short drive to plan her approach.

Claire had her turn signal on and was waiting to enter the underground parking garage of Luke's building when a cherry red Porsche 911 drove out of the garage and turned right.

She pulled in behind him. One good thing about

Bug, he didn't call attention to himself. Still, at the end of the first block, she let a car a slip between them.

Luke took the freeway south, and she pushed Bug hard, so she could keep his red Porsche in sight. He took the West 13th exit and sailed past the funky offbeat shops, hip bars, and coffee houses lining the street. Luke was going to the construction site of the twin condo towers he was building in the Capitol Hill area.

Traffic was light on the surface roads, and she hung back, catching glimpses of him up ahead of her. They passed the Denver Art Museum and two blocks further, Luke turned right. The construction site was ahead on her left. She cruised past and parked a half of a block down and walked to the site.

The churned-up mud from the night's rain had oozed out into the street. She watched as Luke walked on a makeshift sidewalk of plywood boards heading across the muck to a trailer.

He didn't notice her. Her soft-soled shoes were quiet on the makeshift sidewalk. She waited until he was in sight of the construction trailer.

She called his name: "Mr. Backstrom."

He looked up, irritated at the interruption but waited for her to cross the distance between them.

"Yes?" he answered as she came up to him.

Claire identified herself and held up her license.

He looked amused. "I can't imagine why you're here."

"I have a few questions."

"Yeah, well, I'm busy. Make an appointment." He turned away from her.

"I see you have two projects under construction." Claire called to him. "Looks like you've turned the company around."

Luke's fair complexion was flushed pink when he

faced her. His voice tight with anger, he said, "What business is that of yours? Are you still working for the Marsh and Whitley law firm?"

"I do, and I'm investigating Morgan Tutwiler's murder. Did you kill him?"

Claire took a step closer to him. "Or do you know who killed him?"

He put his hands on his hips and bent from the waist.

She could feel his hot breath on her face.

His nostrils flared, and a little tic in his left eye made him look like he was winking. "I was having dinner at the Machias Club. Check with the doorman and the barkeep."

Claire nodded. "Sure, I will. Who else wanted him dead?"

His voice was raw and angry. "Anyone who knew him wanted him dead. I didn't kill him, and you'd better have the decency to leave my mother and me alone."

They had a stare-down for a moment. His lips pressed together in a tight line and his left eyelid twitching furiously.

He broke away first, turning his back to her and heading toward a guy in a hard hat waiting outside the construction trailer. He half-turned toward Claire.

"If I see you again, I'm calling the police and pressing charges for harassment."

Claire walked back to Bug.

Not bad for a first meeting. He was twitchy and tossed out a threat.

CHAPTER SEVEN

Claire fired up Bug and headed to Marvin Arden's wholesale plumbing business near the junction of the freeway and 225.

After Arden's wife died in the bridge collapse, he received a settlement from the wrongful death suit he filed against Tutwiler and Backstrom. He was raising a child on his own and had plenty to be angry about, but Claire knew he hadn't shot Tutwiler. Hawkins would have recognized him. But he might have hired someone to do his dirty work.

Claire parked in front of Arden's business and went inside. His receptionist told her the boss was on the warehouse floor. She took Claire back to his office to wait while she went in search of Arden.

Arden came in as Claire was looking at a picture of his little girl. She reached in her bag for her identification.

"Don't bother. I remember you." He sat in his chair and laced his fingers on the top of the desk. "You're here because Tutwiler got himself killed."

He gestured for her to take a chair.

"I know what you're thinking," Arden said as he sat back in his seat. "And you wouldn't be wrong."

"You wanted Tutwiler dead."

He frowned. "Yeah, I'm fine with him dead. I do feel sorry for his daughter. I have a child of my own who has lost a parent."

Claire started to say something else, and he cut her off.

"You want to check me out," he said. "Go for it. Check my bank records, tap my phone, whatever you need." He paused again. "I didn't kill him, but the world is sure as hell a better place without him. I put the money I got from the lawsuit into my business. You can check that, too."

"So, just to cross the T's and dot the I's – where were you when he was killed?"

"I was down in the Springs at the Expo Center for a vendor's show. I stayed at the Holiday Inn on Palmer Road." He came out from behind the desk and walked toward the door. "If you'll excuse me, I have a business to run and a kid to raise. Look to your heart's content. I have nothing to hide."

Claire found her own way out.

She unlocked Bug and headed to Kwan's to meet Truck. Anyone who had been on the outs with Tutwiler would have an alibi at the ready. They would know someone would come asking questions.

It'd be easy enough to check Arden's whereabouts and Truck would take care of combing through his finances and tracing the windfall he received when his was wife was killed.

Claire drove to the bar trying to think of anyone who had ever said anything good about Morgan Tutwiler and came up with zilch.

Truck's vehicle wasn't in his usual space, dead-center

in front of the bar. She parked in the spot by his usual place.

Claire had just dialed the number for the Holiday Inn on Palmer Road in Colorado Springs when Truck pulled his grumbling massive 4 x 4 into the space beside her.

He got out of his car and popped open Bug's passenger door, sticking his head in but not sitting down.

She held up one finger to keep him from talking

A voice on the other end of the phone answered. "Thank you for calling the Holiday Inn, this is Michael, how may I help you?"

"I'm Mrs. Arden," Claire said. My husband stayed there during the plumber's convention at the Expo a couple of days ago. Marvin left his phone in his room, and we've been waiting for someone to call us and tell us if it's been found. It's an iPhone, and it has a burgundy-colored textured grip cover. He was in room two twenty-three, I think that's what he told me. It's his work phone, and he's desperate for it. Can you help me?"

"Certainly. Give me a minute and I'll check our registrations."

Claire heard tapping on a keyboard.

"Mr. Arden was in room one eighteen. I don't have a message here about a missing phone. Let me talk to my manager. We can recheck the room, but it has been rented. What's a good number to reach you?"

Claire gave him Arden's business phone. "Please let him know as soon as you find anything out and thank you so much. Marvin's such a worrywart." She ended the call and dropped the phone in her bag.

"Babe," Truck said, "I thought we always said we'd invite each other to our weddings. Now you up and married a plumber."

Claire got out of the car, smiling. "You can come to my next wedding. C'mon, I'll buy you a beer."

Truck held the door to Kwan's open, and Claire stood just inside the doorway, letting her eyes adjust from bright sunlight to the dim lighting.

Mi Sun was working behind the bar, and when she saw Truck and Claire, she waved them over.

Claire shot the breeze with Mi Sun while the girl pulled two mugs of beer.

Truck planted a kiss on Mi Sun's cheek, and she giggled.

Claire followed Truck to his booth.

He sat across the table from her and scooted a beer in front her. "Been awhile since I've seen you. You're still looking hot. Who's the plumber dude you're checking up on?"

"Marvin Arden. I need you to find out what he did with the money he got when the suit was settled."

"I remember him," Truck said. "Lost his wife on the bridge." He took a sip of beer. "You think he hired a hitman?"

"Not really, just look into it for me."

"Will do." He grinned. "I got a report on your girl, Amanda."

"Were you able to get into her phone?"

"Babe." He was shaking his head as if she should have known better than to ask that question. "All cell phones got the same flaw in the SS7 system. Yeah, I hacked her phone. Your girl calls just a few personal numbers in Boston that I traced back to the Boston University area. Two belong to women, and the other is a guy's phone in the same area. Maybe a boyfriend?"

"I haven't heard about a boyfriend," Claire said. "Any local calls?"

"A BMW dealership, a decorator, a real estate agent, the limo service, you, and the firm."

"Okay, anything else?"

"Let's start with money," Truck said. "On the first of the month, seven thousand five hundred dollars is deposited into her checking account. At the end of the month, her balance is hovering around zero."

"Where does it go?"

"Ski weekends in the winter. Summer trips to Bar Harbor and the Poconos, shopping in New York. Clothes, movies, restaurants, sports tickets, just stuff."

"That's a lot of walking around money for a college kid. No payments to anyone?"

Truck shook his head. "And no run-ins with the Boston PD or the campus police."

"Wonder if she is paying the expenses for someone to go with her on those trips?"

"You're too nice, Babe." His upper lip curled. "She's an entitled little twat with no idea how the rest of the world lives. She buys one ticket when she goes on trips. Doesn't mean she goes alone, but she's not paying the other guy's way." He took another swig of beer. "She has a Facebook account, but she doesn't post much, and when she does, they're selfies of her and the same couple of women friends. No other social media sites."

Claire drummed her fingers on the table. She didn't have the whole story and it frustrated her. No young woman went off on a weekend in the Poconos alone.

"You want me to toss her apartment?" Truck smiled. "Come on, you want it."

Claire jerked her head up. "She doesn't live in an apartment. She's in a dorm on the university campus."

Truck's deep laugh rumbled. "Babe catch up. Your girl lives in a nice garden apartment two blocks from campus."

"When did she move out of the dorm?"

"She signed a lease four months ago on the apartment."

"No snooping through her apartment or her hotel room here in Denver. It's too risky."

"Okay." Truck shrugged. "Your call. Anyone else you want to know about?"

"Yeah, Luke Backstrom."

"I remember him," Truck said. "Millennium Construction and Tutwiler flamed out together."

"I want to know everything you can dig up on him and his company."

Truck watched her over the rim of his mug. "Consider it done. You think he killed Tutwiler?"

"He'd have to hire someone to do it. Hawkins Reynolds would have recognized him," Claire said. "Speaking of Hawkins, I want you to check his bank records. See if he made a deposit that wasn't a paycheck. He may have partnered with Luke or someone else."

"How soon do you want all this?"

"Tomorrow's good."

"Yeah, right."

She pulled out some cash for the beer and laid it on the table.

He laughed and put two fingers on the bills and pushed them toward her. "Babe, your beer is free at the office."

"Thanks." Claire looked around before leaning over and whispering, "For God's sake, don't break your perfect record and hit a trip wire or an alarm inside some server."

On the way out, she waved to Mi Sun.

She sat in Kwan's parking lot and texted Amanda. *I'm headed your way.*

She pulled out of the parking lot fuming about being caught out not knowing Amanda had new digs in Boston. A year ago, the girl would have been frightened to death to live alone in Boston.

She didn't think the new heiress was alone now.

Who was it and what was the game?

She pulled into the Marriott and left Bug's keys with the valet, telling him she would only be 10 minutes.

She texted Amanda—*I'm in the lobby.*

Two minutes later, Amanda stepped out of the elevator, dressed casually in jeans and a cream-colored sweater over a tucked-in T-shirt. She had a denim jacket thrown over one shoulder, and a sizeable leather bag hooked on the other.

George Ramos stepped out of the elevator behind her.

Amanda stared at Claire. "Does he have to come too?"

"Part of the deal."

"Are we all cramming into your Bug?"

"No, he'll follow us in his own car. Where are we going?"

"Cherry Creek," Amanda said. "Park by the Salon."

"Pick a shop, I'm not having my hair done tonight."

Amanda shrugged. "Okay, your loss. Park by the main entrance."

Claire said to Ramos, who was standing in front of them watching the street. "Are you good with meeting us at the south entrance of Cherry Creek shopping district?"

"No," Ramos said. "Wait for my car to be brought around and I'll follow you."

Claire and Amanda waited in Bug until George's car was delivered and he circled behind them.

They formed a two-car mini motorcade heading for Cherry Creek.

"I went to see Hawkins this morning," Amanda said. "Ramos went with me. He even followed me right to his room and stood outside while I talked to Hawkins. When do I get to ditch him?"

"Not my call. Mr. Marsh hired him."

"Better be soon." Amanda sounded annoyed. "I told Hawkins I wanted him to work for me."

"I bet that made him happy," Claire said looking over her shoulder to change lanes. "Did he agree?"

"Yes." Amanda smiled. "I went car shopping after I saw him."

"Did you find one?"

"A black BMW. As soon as I get the money, I'm picking it up. My trust fund is down to nothing." She threw up her hands. "I know I'm a spender, I've been lectured often enough about it. I have enough to go shopping tonight. I'm not broke, but the BMW has to wait until I get my inheritance."

"How would you have finished school? I mean, with the trust account low and all," Claire asked. Then, "Sorry, that's none of my business."

"I would have to have gone to Daddy and begged. The money would have rolled in. Guilt, you know. He was eaten up with it over what happened to me last year." She picked a piece of lint off her sweater. "He should have been. I could have died, and it was all his fault."

Claire let that pass and changed the subject. "How did it go at the police station?"

"Detective Brewster is hot. Like, really hot. It was a hoot. He thinks I killed him. I would have answered all his questions. Since I didn't do anything, I don't understand what the big deal was with Mr. Marsh shushing me all the time."

"He was looking out for you."

"Detective Brewster kept asking me the same questions over and over, and I kept giving the same answers and then, suddenly he said, 'We're done.'"

Yeah, that sounds like Rafe, Claire thought.

She pulled into a parking spot in front of the south entrance. Ramos pulled in beside her.

"Don't be surprised if the Detective Brewster calls you back in. Cases develop and as more information comes to light the detectives go back and talk to people, so don't freak out."

"You didn't tell me not to worry that he thinks I'm guilty." Amanda pointed out.

They got out of the car and Claire dropped the car keys in her purse. "Good cops let the facts lead them through the case. To him, you're suspect like about a dozen other people."

"If you say so." Amanda headed into the store.

Two HOURS LATER, Amanda was still working her way through the racks like a pro. She'd pull out an item, eye it, reject it or hang it over her arm.

Claire took a chair outside the dressing rooms and settled in for the wait. Ramos stood beside her, his eyes roaming the area.

Occasionally a saleswoman would check on Amanda, bring out discarded items, and return with new things for her to try on. Twice she carried a load of clothes to the register.

Claire's stomach was gnawing its way to her

backbone by the time Amanda called it quits and headed to the register to pay.

Amanda handed over her black American Express card. She'd made a haul: six casual dresses, three sundresses marked down from the summer sales, four pairs of jeans and a couple of pairs of wool pants, assorted shirts in every color, four sweaters, a wool jacket, a navy blazer, and a long black leather coat and a puffer vest.

Ramos and Claire doubled as Sherpas carrying her purchases to Bug. Claire thought they might have to take a running start to stuff them all the in back seat and slam the door shut.

Once in the car, she sneaked a peek at her phone. It was after eight in the evening, and though she was starving, Claire hoped Amanda wouldn't want to have dinner together. She still had work to do.

When they reached the Marriott and Amanda hadn't mentioned having a meal, Claire switched to worrying the girl would give Ramos the slip, meet Lancaster, and have a cozy chat.

More likely, as it was after ten o'clock on the East Coast, Amanda had someone she wanted to talk to and would stay safely tucked up in her room.

Claire parked in the valet circle, and Amanda waited for Ramos to come along the passenger side before she opened her car door. "See you later," she said to Claire, then pointed to the backseat and said to Ramos. "Will you get those for me?"

Claire idled, watching until Amanda and Ramos disappeared into the lobby before

she headed to the hospital to see Hawkins.

On the way, she mulled over a theory lurking in the back of her brain. What if all the people who didn't have enough money to hire a killer pooled their money, hired a hitman, and had Tutwiler killed? Very *Orient Express* style, and there were a lot more than twelve angry people in Denver, so it wouldn't be too expensive for each of them. She dismissed the idea. It would take too much trust between people who didn't know each other well enough to believe no one would break and spill the beans.

Visiting hours ended at eight. Claire stepped off the elevator and waited until the nurse wandered away from the desk. She dashed to Hawkins' room at the end of the corridor by the stairs.

She knocked softly on the door and pushed it open. The only light came from the television.

Backlit by the light spilling in from the hallway, she said, "Hawkins, it's me, Claire."

He clicked the television off. "Come in and turn the light on."

She closed the door before turning on the lights.

His left shoulder was heavily bandaged and in a sling. His hair was lank, and it looked like someone had nicked his chin when they shaved him

His eyes were teary. "Damn, I can't believe he's gone." He thrust his free hand over the bed rail to her.

Claire took his hand. "Are they going to let you out of here soon?"

He squeezed his eyes shut. "Maybe tomorrow. Amanda offered me my old job, but how can I go back there knowing he's never going to be there again?"

"I think Mr. Tutwiler would be happy you're working for his daughter. She needs someone to look out for her."

He let go of her hand and mopped his face with a handful of tissues. "She's in a bad way. I don't know how to help her."

"Maybe just go home and take care of yourself.

Amanda has other people who can help her." She pulled up a chair and sat down. "Do you feel well enough to talk about what happened?"

Hawkins told his story in fits and starts, backing up to add a detail he left out, but in the end, he didn't add anything to the story he told Rafe. When he got to the part where he opened the front door, he broke down, blaming himself for Tutwiler's death.

When he'd composed himself and blown his nose, Claire asked, "Who do you think killed him?"

"I swear I never saw that guy before in my life." He stared at Claire for a moment and blinked. "Someone hired him, didn't they?"

Claire shrugged. "Looks that way to me. Who do you think did it?"

"I don't know. I didn't," and he added quickly, "and Amanda had nothing to do with this."

"Did you know you were included in his will?"

Hawkins nodded. "Yes, he left me two years of salary. Like severance pay, so I'd have time to find work, but I didn't kill him."

"Did you know Amanda receives the rest of the estate?"

"Yes, but you can't think she'd hire someone to murder her own father." His voice cracked. "I know she's saying stuff about her Dad that sounds awful, but she's not herself right now and sometimes she's so childish."

Claire nodded. "I don't want to tire you out and it is after visiting hours, but I have a few more questions. Do you want me to come back?"

"No, stay. I can't sleep anyway. Ask me whatever you want."

"Was anyone threatening Mr. Tutwiler?"

Hawkins shook his head. "Not that I know of. Nothing out of the ordinary was going on."

"No upsetting phone calls? He didn't seem worried about anything?"

"You know he was high strung and always had a bee in his bonnet about something, but he never mentioned a threat to me, and I didn't see anything that made me uneasy."

A nurse had stepped in on crepe-soled shoes, and Claire jumped when she said, "What are you doing in here? Visiting hours are over."

"I'll talk to you later. Get some rest."

Claire sidestepped the nurse and left.

CHAPTER EIGHT

ON THE WAY HOME FROM THE HOSPITAL, CLAIRE CALLED Kirwin to find out if he had wrestled the mattress off the porch and into the house.

"Oh yeah, thanks Pigeon. It's here. You know, I got to find me a new job, something easier on my back," he whined. "But I can keep it up for a while longer. Are you on the way home?"

"Yes, have you eaten? I could pick up Chinese."

"Sounds good."

Wen's was a hole-in-the-wall with great food. It wasn't crowded this time of night, and she was a regular. Wen greeted her by name. They chatted while he packaged her order—egg rolls, fried rice for Kirwin, steamed for her, and beef and broccoli for both.

Within ten minutes, Wen had it boxed and bagged, and Claire was on her way home dreaming of a long hot bath and an early night.

Kirwin met her at the front door and took the bag from her. She was surprised and touched to see he had set the small table in the kitchen complete with silverware and napkins.

He divvied up the egg rolls as she spooned out the rice and beef.

"You look beat. Must have been a hard day. I don't suppose you can talk to me about the case?"

Claire was saved from telling him "No" by her phone ringing.

"Excuse me," Claire said, stepping away from the table. "Hi. What's up?" she said to Rafe.

"Can you meet me at the No Name? We got a second body, and it's connected to the Tutwiler case."

When she hesitated, he added, "I already ordered you a beer."

"Be there in fifteen minutes." She returned to the kitchen. "That was Rafe. I have to go. Will you put my food in the fridge?"

"Sure thing."

———

THE NO NAME BAR was halfway between her duplex and Rafe's craftsman cottage he'd been remodeling for years.

The bar had a couple of pool tables in the back, high-back booths good for private conversations, low lighting, and best of all, the regulars knew each other by the names they said were theirs, even if they weren't necessarily the ones on their birth certificates. No one asked any pesky personal questions.

She parked a block away under a street light and headed on foot for the bar.

Claire pulled open the door, and the thump of heavy bass rumbled in her chest. A gray cloud of cigarette smoke hung over the bar like a low hanging storm cloud.

All the bar stools were taken, and most of the

tables had two to three customers. Rafe waved from a booth in the back as far away from the band as possible.

She slid onto the cracked Naugahyde seat across from him.

She took a sip of the pale ale he'd ordered her.

She leaned across the table to be heard. "What happened?"

"A man's body was found a couple of hours ago at Sue's Truckstop out on Interstate 70. A kitchen worker taking out the trash found him behind a dumpster, shot twice, once in the chest and another in the head. Dead around twenty-four hours."

"And?" she asked.

"And what?"

"I wouldn't be here if you didn't think there was a connection to the Tutwiler case. What's the rest of the story?"

"The prints on the shells match the prints at the Tutwiler house."

Claire sat back in the booth with a satisfied smile. Finally, a break. "Who's the dead guy?"

Rafe shook his head. "No damn clue. I wasn't on this case at the get-go. It was Red Stilinski's. He wasted time working it as a sex deal gone bad. He thought the dead guy was a lot lizard servicing truckers. I didn't get the call until the prints matched."

"Why did Red think it was a sex killing?"

"Because the Vic was only wearing his boxers and socks."

Claire's eyes narrowed as she pieced it together. "The truck stop victim had no clothes, and five miles away, Tutwiler's killer is wearing clothes too small for him. Why didn't you just say the truck stop vic is probably the Big Pies delivery guy?"

Rafe put his beer down. "Because I can't prove it—yet."

"Whose case is this now? Yours or Red's?"

Rafe dragged a hand through his unruly hair. "Mine. Something's gotta give with Red. He's dragging the Sixth's clearance rate down. Beekman's pissed and on everyone's ass about our stats."

"Is Red mad about losing the case?"

"He's not happy about it, but mad is too strong a word. Red's not a good fit for homicide. He wants to work eight to five and go home."

Claire didn't comment on the strife in the Sixth Division. "Do you have a copy of the John Doe's picture I can have?"

"I'll email it to you. We're checking missing persons and my guys are asking the Big Pies' managers if any delivery guy is missing."

"Wouldn't each store know if someone was missing, because the money bag hadn't come in?"

He shook his head. "Hell no, that would be way too easy. The managers have such a high turnover rate of drivers, they can't look at the picture of the dead man and say for sure if he drives for them or not. And then, just to make it more difficult, it turns out it's not unusual for a driver to make his final run and not bring the money bag in until his next shift. Against corporate policy, but some managers let it slide."

"Anything useful from the people who work in the diner? Or the truckers?"

"Not yet. The dumpsters sit way out at the end of the lot behind the kitchen. No one has any business over there except to dump garbage, and the diner didn't waste money putting cameras on their dumpsters. We're running checks on everyone."

"What about other security camera footage?"

"Yeah, we're looking. It's possible to cut through the vacant land adjacent to the truck stop and come up on the backside of the dumpsters and not be seen, but that lot's so full of underbrush and every kind of trash imaginable, I don't see us getting tread prints."

"Never is easy. What did Nicole find on the traffic cameras around Tutwiler's house?"

"There's footage of the Big Pies car on I-70 and turning in and out of Tutwiler's neighborhood, but we don't have an identifiable picture of the driver. He was slumped down in the front seat with the brim of his hat sitting on his eyebrows. He knew about traffic cameras, he kept his head tucked low."

Claire sipped her beer, then sat back. "Play along with me for a moment. If Tutwiler's killer murdered the guy at the truck stop, I bet he walked through the brush to the dumpsters. Way to risky too drive your car onto the property covered in security cameras. That means he left his own car within walking distance of the dumpster." She thought for a moment. "Those abandoned warehouses in the industrial area between North Broadway and East Fifty-Sixth are an easy walk to the truck stop, and not too far from Tutwiler's house. After he killed Tutwiler, he would have needed a place to dump the Big Pies car fast and get the heck out of Dodge in his own vehicle."

Rafe sat back and folded his arms over his chest. "Or he could have had a partner who helped him out with the vehicles."

"Maybe, or it could be that Tutwiler's killer and the truck stop victim were partners," Claire said. "And once the killer got the uniform and car, he didn't need the partner, so he killed him."

Rafe shrugged. "Maybe this, maybe that, but the simplest explanation is when a man orders a pizza, a driver shows up with a pizza. The truck stop vic was just the unlucky son-of-a bitch who delivered a pie to a killer who needed a disguise. And the man who shot him and Tutwiler was hired by the person who had the most to gain."

Claire raised her index finger. "You're talking about Amanda?"

Rafe didn't answer.

"How are you linking Amanda to the body behind the dumpster?" she asked. "The Boston PD checked; she was in class from five to eight that evening. Her professor remembers seeing her."

"She does have a great alibi," Rafe agreed, "but you're dancing around the fact she could have hired someone."

"Oh c'mon, Rafe. Can you see her doing that? Really? You talked to her. She's a sheltered rich girl, squanders money on expensive stuff, and suddenly, she goes shopping for a killer? What does she do? Call the University Career Center and ask if they have any assassins for hire? It doesn't fit."

He grinned. "You don't sound objective. Is your boss jockeying to manage her affairs?"

"Yes, he wants her business," Claire admitted. "And he has it . . . for now."

"Then you have too much skin in the game to be objective."

"I know her better than you do," Claire said.

Rafe's phone buzzed.

When she realized it was a private conversation, she got up to give him some space.

He motioned for her to sit.

She could tell from his side of the conversation that he was talking to Lily, his thirteen-year-old daughter.

Rafe and his ex, Diane, passed Lily back and forth

on weekends and holidays like a football. Rafe did score extra time with Lily whenever Diane was in rehab for her opioid addiction.

Rafe listened more than he talked. He put his phone down after agreeing to something Lily wanted and leaned his head back on the booth. "Lily wants to come and stay with me. Her Mom is acting crazy again."

Rafe was only fifteen years older than Claire, but tonight each year was etched on his face.

Claire asked if she could help.

This time Rafe shook his head.

She sat across from him and gave him space. The two of them could talk about anything, his addicted ex-wife, her latest dating disaster, Lily, Kirwin, it didn't matter. If only she'd had that with the guy she wasted a year on. But no, it had been about the sex. She could hardly wait to be flat on her back with her legs in the air, but when the sex was over, it was like canoodling with a refrigerator.

Rafe rubbed the back of his neck and sighed. "Di may be hitting the damn pills again."

"I'm sorry. If you need help with Lily, give me a call."

"Yeah, thanks. Family is fun, isn't it?" His smile was tight. "How's yours?"

"Kirwin's sleeping on his new twin bed mattress."

His phone vibrated.

"It's Lily again," Rafe said. He listened, promised he was on his way, and ended the call. He dialed 911, identified himself and gave them Diane's address. "I'm on my way. The child in the house is my daughter."

He grabbed his coat and slid out of the booth. "Diane's passed out and hit her head." He hurried to the door.

Claire rummaged in her bag and found her wallet.

She put a twenty on the bar and caught the bartender's eye and pointed.

By the time she reached Bug, a quick shower was drenching the city, and Rafe's brake lights were twin red dots disappearing into the dark.

Claire cranked up Bug and headed home. The quick shower had softened to a gray mist shot through with pools of yellow light from the streetlamps.

Bug's heater trickled a thin stream of warm air over her feet. She was going to have to splurge on a new heater for Bug before the snows came. There must be money somewhere in the budget.

She turned on Zuni, and her lights flashed over the gray sedan parked on the opposite side of the street from the duplex. She slowed when she passed it and caught the plate number.

She pulled in her drive and grabbed the pad she kept stuffed between the front seats and jotted down the number.

Truck called her before she opened her front door. She let herself in listening to Truck talk.

"I don't have everything you want but, I got some information on Hawkins Reynolds. I'm emailing it to you also, but here's the guts of what I found. The guy doesn't own anything of value but his car. He has a little over two thousand in his checking account, about fifteen thou in savings, and a nice chunk in a retirement account held in Tutwiler Industries retirement plan. He's not making big cash withdrawals, and his cards are paid off every month. No red flags on his phone. Most of the calls are to the Bryant woman. I had a look at her finances, too. She's hanging onto the high life by her fingertips."

Claire listened, while going through the house flipping on the lights.

"And I checked out Marvin Arden," Truck said. "Since his wife died and he got the money, he's doubled the size of his warehouse here in Denver and opened a second location in Colorado Springs. An expansion like that eats up his profit. He's making money, but it's all going back into his business. Babe, you owe me a steak dinner for the rush job."

"Yeah, pick a time," she said before hanging up, thinking unless a big cash deposit was made in Hawkins' account after the estate was probated, she had no evidence he was involved in Tutwiler's murder, and she was right. Marvin Arden didn't hire the killer.

They were 24 hours into the Tutwiler investigation, racing the clock to solve it before 48 hours past. After that, the clearance rate tumbled.

Rafe was right. Amanda had the most to gain financially, but Claire would gamble her job the girl was innocent.

Someone would talk. Lonely as having a secret is, it's harder to keep it to yourself.

CHAPTER NINE

MILLENNIUM CONSTRUCTION WAS ON THE THIRD FLOOR of a swanky downtown high-rise. Luke was first into work like he always was, so he could stare-shame his staff to their cubicles when they filtered in carrying doughnuts and coffee, wasting time bullshitting. His father had been lackadaisical with the employees. Not him. He ran a tight ship.

Once his people were at work in their cubicles, Luke went to the office he inherited from his Dad. Two floor-to-ceiling glass walls forming a ninety-degree angle corner, one looking west at the mountains, and the other north into the financial center of Denver.

Only Luke and the paper pushers worked out of the downtown office. The hard work was done by men who worked out of construction trailers plunked down in mud at the sites. Luke used the plush digs to woo investors and impress clients.

On the top of his desk was the daily calendar his assistant prepared as the last task of her workday. She had penciled in time for a meeting at one of the building sites.

Luke liked to get out and visit the construction sites, shoot the bull with the workers, and watch big equipment gnaw holes in the earth. The concrete trucks, their backup alarms beeping, pouring thousands of tons of concrete were the sweet sounds of money being made.

He hoped Detective Brewster wouldn't track him to the construction site with more questions. Thirty-six hours after Tutwiler's death, and he'd already been questioned twice by Brewster. Once at the cop shop and once in his office.

Sam Burnside had done a good job coaching Luke and Sonja for the interviews. In their prep sessions, Burnside baited them with emotionally loaded questions, picked apart their answers, badgered them, then smiled, and asked the same questions again.

It was good training for what Detective Brewster dished out. He picked through all the financial details of Millennium's near collapse and pounded Luke with questions about what he thought and what his emotions were.

Burnside had called Brewster's tactics "stress testing."

Luke called it being a dickhead.

Luke was sure Brewster thought he and Sonja were the perfect pair to hang the murder on, but the cops didn't have a shred of evidence. So far, he and Sonja had hung tight, but he wasn't sure his mom could hold it together much longer.

Sonja doubled down on her Xanax the morning she was questioned, and Burnside later told Luke his mother didn't break down, even when Brewster thrust a photo of Dave's mangled car resting on its hood at the bottom of the mountain. Burnside said his mother tapped the picture and said, "Dave always loved that car." Yeah, she had been medicated to the gills.

Even a nosy private investigator working for Tutwiler's law firm had been sniffing around, but he managed to keep it together with the Callahan woman, too.

Luke had finally worked his way around to coming to grips with the idea that his 50K didn't buy Tutwiler's murder. The killing was too impulsive and sloppy to have come from the same people who had given him such detailed directions on how to deliver the money.

Those same smart people left him with a big problem. They had his cell phone number and someone out there was walking around knowing he'd paid to have Tutwiler killed.

A thing like that could come back to bite a man in the ass.

After Callahan questioned him, he thought about hiring a private investigator to hunt down the person he paid the 50K to, but there was no guarantee of confidentiality, and he sure as hell wasn't confiding in Burnside.

Luke was beginning to search everyone's eyes for a tell that they were the one who knew his secret. He was acting as crazy as his mother.

He was going to have to do something with his Mom soon. She was increasingly emotional and secretive. She hung up her phone when he came into the room. Other times, she let it go to voicemail, and Sonja had never been able to ignore a ringing telephone.

Since they were on a family cell phone plan, he'd checked the bill. He saw she was getting phone calls from a number in Weld County. He asked her who she was talking to and she told him an old girlfriend.

She was a terrible liar. She hadn't lived in Weld

County in decades. Sure, she had the occasional call from Weld, but the ones on the bill were from a different number and coming every day.

Sonja was becoming a liability.

She wouldn't hold up under questioning if Brewster changed his mind and pulled her in for a second chat. Luke suggested a stay at the spa she liked down in Santa Fe, but she balked, saying her place was with him.

Luke needed to get her out of town.

She was drinking too much, and she was a maudlin, sloppy drunk. Last night at dinner, she was already soused when he arrived, and she kept knocking them back. Babbling on and on about her love for him and all the things she gave up for him—then declaring it was all worth it. She talked of her dead parents, her longing for what might have been and the terrible guilt of what she'd done.

What the hell was she feeling guilty about? Did she have Tutwiler killed?

Couldn't be. What were the chances they both hired someone to kill him? Zilch. Totally improbable.

It was just the booze and pills talking. She couldn't have done it. She wouldn't know where to begin to hire a hit man.

Last night, he took advantage of her drunkenness. He'd hit her up for more money, working it hard, reminding her how hard Dave had slaved to repair their reputation and rebuild trust in the company. He'd laid it on thick, pointing out he was doing what his Dad wanted, and the company was on the upswing.

Lord how she loved a turnaround story.

She started bawling like a baby. Talking about how Dave killed himself because Tutwiler ruined their company.

Horseshit. His Dad killed himself because he

couldn't stand the pity in peoples' eyes. The coward drove off the pass and left him holding the bag.

And because dear old Dad offed himself, they couldn't collect on his life insurance policies.

Way to stick it to me, Dad.

He deserved Sonja's money. He and the company were putting food on the table and paying her bills.

But she stood firm. No more money. She claimed the check she'd given him right after Dave died was her inheritance from her dad.

He certainly had been surprised the day she handed him the check. He thought her family was dirt poor. But he didn't look a gift horse in the mouth.

Now, he needed her to get her checkbook out and write another one. Coming up empty-handed was going to be a problem.

His gambling debt was substantial, no way around it, but he was a lucky guy. He would hit it big and get Donovan off his back. In the meantime, until his luck changed, he needed to cash to stave off another nasty encounter with Donovan.

What his Mom didn't know was he'd invested the company's cash and part of what she gave him with a broker who approached him with a sweetheart deal. An investment guaranteed to double his money in six months. *Guaranteed.* Brett Allen Buckner handpicked the investors he invited in to the deal. Buckner had answered all Luke's questions and after they met, senior advisors called from Buckner Investments to see if Luke had additional questions.

Luke checked them out on the web. Buckner had a very professional website set up so clients could buy and sell through the Internet.

Buckner and a senior advisor took him out for drinks and dinner at the Highlander Club, using the opportunity to blow warm air up his pants leg, telling Luke that Buckner had handpicked him to be in on this deal because he was such a smart young man.

The next day Luke moved the cash to Buckner. The company set up an online account for him. It was fun checking his account, watching his money grow with the close of each day on the Exchange.

Millennium finished a small project and Luke was ballsy enough to invest the profit with Buckner.

It was wonderful until the Buckner website went down, and Luke couldn't access his account or get in contact with Buckner, or any of those ever-so-friendly senior advisors.

He jumped online and did some deeper research. It turned out Buckner Investments wasn't registered with the U.S. Securities and Exchange Commission.

Bye-bye money.

Luke got up and grabbed his coat. He had to get out of the office.

He paused at his assistant's desk and told her he'd be gone a couple of hours visiting sites.

Luke took the elevator to the executive level of the parking garage where his Porsche sat safe from the dings and dents of careless drivers. When he stepped off the elevator, his red 911 sat gleaming.

He fired her up and roared toward the exit.

He'd work out the money problems. He'd graduated Wharton. He was a lucky guy. He wasn't riding this company into the poorhouse.

It was a beautiful fall morning, a great day to be outside. The sky was a clear blue, and the air had the scent of dry leaves.

He kept the Porsche to the legal limit until he reached the freeway, then he let the horses out to run. The Porsche whipped past a battered Jeep. Luke caught the guy's look of surprise in his rearview mirror.

The morning rush was down to a trickle of cars on the freeway. The Porsche's gears moved smoothly under his hands, and he slipped into his boyhood fantasy.

He was a race car driver. On the track, running the biggest race of his life.

He downshifted on the turn.

Whizzed past his pit crew.

Flew past the lead car.

His fans howled his name as he crossed the finish line.

God, how he loved daydreaming he was a race car phenom. Not a guy saddled with an ailing business and a loose-lipped drunk for a mother.

He reminded himself, he wasn't an *ordinary* man. Maybe his dick was failing him. Maybe it would turn out he hired the Apple Dumpling gang to kill Tutwiler. But he was sure of one thing: He knew how to make money.

The problem was, it took money to make money. He'd been counting on his mother to cough up a chunk of change. Now, he'd have to convince her to sell the house and downsize.

He downshifted and slowed to the exit to the site where he was building the most significant project Millennium had ever signed. The Market on Main.

A multi-use destination shopping and living area on West 32nd near Interstate 25, the space was already leased to boutiques and anchor stores, bars, restaurants, movie theaters, and even an outdoor amphitheater. Building the Market would make his reputation and be the comeback the business needed.

What a stroke of luck to be partnered with a big commercial real estate developer from back East. The deal to build the Market had been in the works for nearly a year before he signed the it with Ingram and Mellor, but it could all go down the crapper in a flash without money to pay his crews.

He idled in front of the worksite. The men were doing pad work. Not much to see except big machines pushing dirt around but being on the job site beat the hell out of sitting in the office worrying about his gambling debt and his tanked investment.

His phone rang through the Porsche's Bluetooth system. James Allerton from Ingram and Mellor was on the line.

Luke hurried through the pleasantries. Allerton was clueless about construction, and Luke couldn't really put his finger on what Allerton's contribution to the company was.

Allerton announced he was going to be in town on other business and wanted to visit The Market site. "Just wanting to check to make sure all the amendments to the plans went to the construction foreman and he's good with the changes."

Luke made murmuring noises of agreement to meet him at the site and got off the phone as fast as possible.

He resented the intrusion. Allerton was an idiot. All the principals had signed off on each change to the building plan as the changes were made and then signed the agreement to build. Allerton thought Millennium's construction foreman had some say-so in plan changes? Hardly. That was made at a level way above a foreman working on site.

The phone call had him steaming. Now, he'd have to waste a couple of hours taking Allerton around the construction site, probably feed him a meal, and absolutely nothing would come of their meeting.

Why would Allerton fly halfway across the country

to peer into a hole in the ground? Luke could have sent pictures or a video.

Then, cold shot down his spine.

Allerton was Ingram's lackey. Ingram had said as much in one of the executive meetings. What if Ingram had some doubts and was sending Allerton to snoop?

Just what he needed, something else to worry about.

He moved the Porsche to the opposite side of the street from the building site. He'd still have to run her through the wash. The earthmovers were sending clouds of brown dust into the air.

He took the time to change from his loafers to a pair of old hiking boots he kept in the back seat.

The construction supervisor recognized his car and met him when he was crossing the churned-up field heading to the trailer. The supervisor glad-handed him with assurances the project was on schedule, and he had no problems.

Luke told him to expect a visit from Allerton. Then, Luke did a walk-around with the supervisor. Satisfied the project looked like it was on-time, he drove back to the office and worked steadily into the early evening.

He slipped his laptop in his briefcase and passed through the darkened reception area. Like always, he was the last to leave. Only the security lights his assistant left on were burning.

He left thinking he couldn't stomach the thought of another evening with his mom, her crying and talking nonsense.

He'd had a good day at the office. His energy level was high, and he wanted to ride the crest. If he went home, Sonya would drag him down with her blues.

He called her with his apologies, telling her he had to work late, and he felt no guilt about the lie or her disappointment. He was taking care of himself.

What he needed was to blow off steam at the Machias Club. His step was light as he headed to the garage. He roared down the ramp heading to the club.

Twenty minutes later, Luke rang the Machias' doorbell, a small brass button set in a black marble plaque with raised brass letters spelling out the club's name.

He was a legacy member, following in his father and grandfather's footsteps. Many of the members were descendants of the Railroad Kings. When the '59ers found gold in the Rockies, their forefathers built the railroad connecting Denver to the Pacific and made great fortunes. Those first scions of wealth patterned the club after a posh men's club in London.

Cold rain dripped down Luke's neck as he waited to be admitted. He pulled his coat collar up higher.

The old members insisted the club keep to the original ritual of admittance, and it drove him and the younger members nuts. Waiting in a cold rain while some elderly man looked him over was a ridiculous waste of time. When the old farts died, his generation would drag the Machias into the 3rd millennium.

The small wooden slider in the door squeaked as it rolled aside. Two black eyes stared out at Luke.

Then, the heavy door swung open.

"Good evening, Mr. Backstrom. May I take your coat?"

Luke handed it over, along with his winter gloves. How idiotic was this?

The perimeter of the building and the porches were covered by cameras as were all the betting areas in the club. Well-paid men watched all the monitors.

They knew he was at the damn door before he rang the bell.

He walked into the gathering room. It hadn't changed a bit since he'd first come with his grandfather. Well-oiled dark brown leather furniture arranged to encourage private conversations sat on the thick red carpet. Time and cigar smoke had blackened the walnut woodwork. Lamps cast a pale-yellow wash of light over the room.

Luke walked through to the gambling rooms. He was a craps man, but he played the roulette wheel, the blackjack tables, and if his streak of luck was nowhere to be found, he'd bet on the dogs and horses.

Upstairs, there were the discreet services of beautiful women. Which was a godsend for Luke, as he seemed unable to get it up under any other circumstances. Not since the unfortunate moment at his aunt's house when he left the dinner table to get something from his coat pocket, only to find his lovely fiancée screwing his best man on the guests' coats.

After that unfortunate sight, his dick shriveled and failed him with any decent woman. His dick did seem to view dipping into a whore as more of a business deal and rose to the occasion.

Luke exchanged his cash for chips. Just the anticipation associated with that simple act thrilled him.

He walked around the room scrutinizing the action, hunting for a hot table. Lady Luck was riding on his shoulder.

Luke heard a whoop and pulled up short by a craps table. A stickman was pushing a pile of chips to a roller. Players were standing shoulder to shoulder, drinks all around, and bets went down as soon as the croupier cleared the table.

This was the hot game he'd been looking for. He'd

be a winner tonight. He pushed his way to place at the table.

Dark thoughts crowded in reminding him of his gambling debt.

You better be lucky, or your ass is grass.

He'd been feeling a decided chill when Mick Donovan came around the tables, and Donovan was showing a vicious side he'd never seen.

Luke shut his negative thoughts down. If he gave them free rein, Lady Luck would fly away.

He sorted his chips and put them in the rack. He'd put his best game on the felt and everything would turn out fine. He could feel it.

A cocktail waitress sauntered up, and Luke ordered a Jameson on the rocks.

He placed a pass line bet and watched the dice tumble down the table. The house edge was less than two percent. His bet wasn't going to make or break him. He was warming up, getting the feel of the table before he put the real money down.

The cocktail waitress returned with his drink, and he chugged it and asked for another.

He was ready.

He placed a hardway bet. Crapped out. First real bet at the table and he was a loser. He switched to betting six and eight until he built his stack of chips.

The waitress returned with another Jameson.

He tried his luck on single roll bets, went for the ace deuce. All he needed was to shoot a sweet one and a two on the dice. With a fifteen to one payout, he'd clean up and get out of here.

The shooter rolled a six and a nine.

The stickman swept his money from the table, and the guy next to him was stacking twenty-dollar chips in the chip rack.

With a horns bet, his odds were better. If a shooter rolled a two, three, eleven or twelve, he'd get paid.

The shooter rolled a five.

The player handed Luke the dice. It was his turn to shoot. Maybe he should take his chips, cash out and go home.

He glanced at his meager row of chips in the rack. He might as go for broke and bet it all.

"Six hardway," Luke said.

The stickman put Luke's chips in the proposition section of the table.

Luke blocked out the noise and concentrated. A single flick of his wrist and a roll of the dice, and he'd be counting his cash, or leaving with his tail between his legs.

Luke turned the dice in his hands until he was staring at two threes. Six was his lucky number. If he shot a six hardway, the payment would be nine to one.

He blew on the dice, his eyes trained on the back-left side of the table. Bouncing them off the side, the odds of rolling a six were better.

He'd done it before and tonight, he'd do it again.

He took a deep breath and cast the dice. While they were airborne, he held his breath. When they bounced off the back of the table, he chanted: *Six. Six. Six.*

The players around him leaned in for a better look. He felt the hot breath of people behind him, leaning in for better look.

The dice tumbled to a stop.

"Nine," called the stickman. A collective groan rose from the players. The stickman raked the table clean.

Luke nodded to the group and retreated to the bar. He was nursing a drink when Mick Donovan joined him.

"Bad luck for you tonight." Donovan sat on the stool

beside Luke and signaled the bartender to bring him a drink.

Luke pegged Donovan to in his seventies, but he still carried himself straight as a board and looked like he worked out hard. He'd heard the whispers that Donovan worked for Checkers Smaldone back in the seventies when Checkers and his brother were the kings of the northern Colorado rackets.

The bartender set a fresh drink in front of Donovan.

"How's business?" he asked Luke.

On the heels of his losses at the table, the last thing he wanted to do was talk to Donovan. He hunched over his drink. "Nothing to complain about."

Donovan took a swig of his drink. He rubbed two fingers through the wet circle his glass made on the bar. "I hear it's real pretty up on the Old Ute Trail."

Luke froze.

"A person could hike up there and never see a soul. Damn good place to do some business a man wants to keep secret. Been up there, Luke?"

Luke stared down into his drink. "Never have."

Donovan stood up, grinning. He clamped his hand on Luke's shoulder, keeping it there too long. Then he leaned in close and said, "You stay outta trouble now."

Luke watched Donovan's back disappear into the crowd. His hands were shaking so hard, his signature on the bar chit was unreadable. Sweating like a racehorse, he forced himself not to run for the door. He didn't take a deep breath until he was in the car.

My God, he'd hired Donovan to kill Tutwiler. What would Donovan ask to keep his mouth shut?

CHAPTER TEN

CLAIRE WOKE AT SIX, AND HER FIRST THOUGHT WAS THAT today marked thirty-six hours since the murder. The clock was ticking.

She was ready for work and in the kitchen pouring her coffee by the time Kirwin stirred. He pulled himself up and got to his feet.

"Morning. I'll bring you a cup of coffee." She filled her travel mug and poured a cup for him.

Kirwin heaved himself into the chair and held his hands out for the cup. "Thanks. I slept like a baby. Don't you worry none. I'll pay you back for the bed."

Claire squeezed his shoulder. "See you later." She left thinking she should have kissed him on his forehead, but she couldn't imagine that kind of intimacy between them.

Claire was on Zuni heading to work when she called Rafe. "Hope I didn't wake you."

"I haven't been to bed yet," he said. "We got ID on the truck stop vic. Jerome Matthews, he drove for the Big Pies on South Downing. His wife called the station this morning when his picture hit the early news shows."

"Why didn't she report him missing earlier?" Claire asked. "It'd been hours since she'd seen him."

"She was afraid to call the cops. She and her son are in the country on visas. They immigrated from Somalia."

"What's her name?"

"Alima Saad Matthews."

"Was Matthews here on a visa?"

"No, he was born in the states. We brought Alima in, and she didn't recognize Tutwiler's picture or name."

"If she has a visa, why was she afraid."

"Because she and the child are Yemeni. They don't trust the police and they're afraid of being sent home. Did you need something?"

"Yeah, a favor," Claire said, and then asked him to run the plate of the gray sedan.

"Sure, I'll get someone on it."

"Thanks, how's the family doing?"

"Di overdosed. Her parents want me to convince her to go back into rehab."

"Why you?"

"Because it's a nasty freakin' job, and Tom and Gena don't want to make their precious daughter mad at them. They've filed a petition for temporary custody of Lily, claiming my work schedule makes me unfit."

Wow, he was having a bad day.

"That's ballsy to ask you to convince Diane to go to rehab and then turn around and try to get custody of Lily."

"That's Di's parents," he said. "I'll call you when I hear about the plate."

"Thanks for the favor."

Claire took the elevator up to her office. She closed the door behind her. A lot of off-the-wall ideas she chased to ground during an investigation turned up nothing, and she kept them to herself. On the rare times she struck gold, she was happy to spread the news and pat herself on the back for her fabulous intuition. That probably wouldn't happen this time, but who knew?

What was rattling around in her brain now was the question: Had Tutwiler done business with a foreign-owned company? Is that why he and Matthews were murdered?

A quick search of Tutwiler Industries in Dun & Bradstreet, Moody's, and Hoover's Profiles turned up no sign Tutwiler had ever partnered with a foreign company.

This was one out-there idea no one had to know about.

She thumbed through her contacts to Nicole Keller's number.

"Hey, Nicole, it's Claire. Got a minute to talk about the Tutwiler case?"

"Sure," Nicole said. "It's bogged down," she whispered. "Listen, Brewster's head isn't in the game. I know the two of you are tight, so maybe you can put the word to him that people are noticing his family problems are affecting his job."

From the way Rafe had described Beekman, Claire thought his Captain would throw him under the bus to save his own skin if the brass needed a scapegoat. "Thanks for telling me. I'll see what I can do."

"Good." Claire heard the relief in Nicole's voice.

"Beekman's got a bug up his ass about this case, and

it's no help that the Lancaster woman puts us on the front page of the *Post* every day."

"You're right about that," Claire said, thinking of her problems with Amanda and the press. "Hey, do you know if your computer guys have taken apart Huber's computer?"

"Yeah, they found the email he sent his company reporting the broken camera on the gate. He was telling the truth about that, but that's not all they found. He was using the laptop like it was his personal machine. Playing video poker, surfing porn. He also did his banking on it. He's broke and behind on his credit cards and car payments."

"Any big deposits?" Claire asked.

"No, just his paychecks."

"Okay, thanks. Maybe when this settles down, we can have lunch."

"Sure, sounds great."

Claire hung up and opened the Tutwiler file, skimming the evidence and eyewitness statements and the motives and alibis. There were too many loose ends and holes in the case. She'd needed to turn up the pressure and ask more questions.

She checked her email and found Rafe's message from last night. She printed a copy of Jerome Matthews' picture and stuck it in her file.

Then, she scoured the web for photographs of her most likely suspects, and it wasn't hard to find pictures. Lots of people post their pictures on social media, and companies post employees' photos on their websites. Newspaper archives were a goldmine of images.

An hour of searching and right-clicking and printing and she had photos of Hawkins Reynolds, Hal Huber, Amanda Tutwiler, Sonja and Luke Backstrom, and Jerome Matthews. She also had the police artist sketch from Hawkins and Huber's interviews—which was so generic it could have been any guy in town. She put them in a folder and stuffed it in her bag.

On her way out, she stopped at Jenny's desk.

"Do you know when Mr. Marsh will be in?"

"He's in court until late morning."

"Can you pencil me into his schedule? Say, noon?"

"Sure thing."

Claire headed for the parking garage.

SHE ARRIVED at the Big Pies on South Downing where Matthews had worked. It was too early for the store to be open, but through the glass front, she saw the crew was busy chopping mounds of vegetables.

She knocked on the door and held her PI license flat against the glass. A young guy dried his hands on his apron, curious enough to walk out from behind the counter for a closer look. She pantomimed opening the door.

He held up one finger and walked behind the counter into the kitchen.

A middle-aged man in a polo shirt and pressed khakis came to the door with the younger guy tagging behind.

Once again Claire held her license up to the glass.

Khaki Pants unlocked the front door and partially opened it. "Is this about Jerome? I already told the police all I know."

"I'm Claire Callahan, a private investigator working his case." A small fib. She was working the Tutwiler case, but decided not to split hairs. Jerome's death was a part of her case.

"I'm Joe Calhoun, I manage this place. Jerome was a

good guy, worked hard to support his wife and kid." He ran his hand through his hair. "I don't want you upsetting my guys. They have it in their head some asshole is shooting pizza delivery guys for sport. One of them already quit this morning. Left saying working here wasn't worth dying for."

"I understand, but it's important. Could I ask you a few questions?"

He didn't look happy about it, but he waved her toward a table.

She smiled at him across the table. "Can you tell me about the evening Matthews died?"

Calhoun snorted. "Every night's the same. Assholes and elbows to closing time. Hang on a sec." He got up and walked away.

He came back with a laptop. He tapped a few keys, scrolled down the page and then turned the machine so Claire could read it.

"See—there's the order. It came in at four thirty-five, and there's a note to deliver to the red rig parked over near the dumpsters. Matthews left with the pie at five-fifteen."

"Thanks, that's helpful." Claire pulled the folder from her bag and fanned out the photos on the tablecloth. "Do you recognize any of these people?"

He took his time looking at each one, then tapped Matthews' picture. "That's Jerome. I don't know the rest."

"Can your crew take a look?"

Calhoun got up. "We have to open this store in an hour." He thought about it for a moment, then nodded, and called the crew over from their work.

Claire got up and stepped back. They crowded around the table. "Just take your time and have a look at each of them."

Most were curious, a couple looked antsy, but no one recognized anyone but Matthews.

"Thanks, guys." Calhoun clapped his hands together. "Let's get ready to open this place."

He looked at Claire. "Sorry we couldn't be of more help."

"Thanks for the time." Claire slipped the pictures in the folder. She gave him her business card. "If you remember anything about Jerome that might be helpful, give me a call. Oh, I almost forgot. Do you know where he lived?"

"Two blocks south in the Iconic Apartments."

"Thanks. And I'm sorry about Matthews." She turned and pushed the door open, walking into the bright sunshine. She drove south.

The Iconic Village sat on the corner two blocks from the pizza place just like Calhoun said. There was nothing iconic about the place. Slapping the name Iconic on the apartments didn't mask the fact they'd been built in the sixties and apparently never updated. The psychedelic orange and lime-green paint had faded under the Denver sun, and the roofline looked like a swaybacked mare.

The manager's office was plainly marked. A reed-thin man was standing behind the counter reading a newspaper. He looked up at her and raised one eyebrow. "Can I help you?"

She held up her PI license. "I'm here to speak with Alima Matthews. Which apartment is hers?"

"I don't give out my renters' addresses."

Claire smiled. "I'm here to help Ms. Matthews." She pulled out her wallet and put a twenty on the counter.

He didn't make a move to pocket it.

She placed a second twenty on top of it. "Ms. Matthews' apartment number?"

"Two-thirteen," he said, the bills disappearing off the counter.

The Matthews' apartment was on the second floor, the third from the end. A narrow concrete walkway ran in front of the units connecting to staircases on each end. At one time, the doors had been painted bright neon colors—green, orange, pink, or yellow, and repeated in sequence. Alima's door was a faded yellow. The curtains were closed over the front window.

Claire knocked.

The curtains swayed, but the door stayed shut.

Claire knocked again. "Ms. Matthews, I'm Claire Callahan. I'm not with the police. I work for a law firm. I'm might be able to help."

From inside, a baby wailed.

She knocked again.

The chain rattled off, and the door came open a few inches.

Alima was dressed in black with a bright blue hijab covering her hair.

A crying boy, maybe a year old, clutched two handfuls of her hijab in his little fists. He doubled up his knees and rubbed his face into his mother's shoulder.

"May I come in?"

Alima stepped back, opened the door wider, and Claire slipped through. The furniture was meager and tatty. Two straight-back chairs, a milk crate doing service as a coffee table, and the baby's crib along the far wall. The entire apartment was two rooms. A bedroom opened directly off the front room. The dark brown carpet was worn, little brown tufts sticking out of the black backing. No plants, pictures, or personal knickknacks gave the place any warmth.

Alima gestured to a chair.

She and Alima sat across from each other. The boy quit crying and turned his head, surveying Claire with big, curious dark eyes.

Claire smiled.

He hid his face in his mother's shoulder.

"He's beautiful. How old is he?" Claire asked.

"One, his name is Emir," she said.

"I'm sorry for your loss. I'm trying to find the man who killed your husband."

Her eyes filled with tears. "Jerome was a good man."

"His boss thought so too. How did you meet?"

"He taught English classes in the mornings at the Lutheran church. I was his student."

Pizza delivery man at night, English teacher in the mornings. Matthews had been a hard worker.

"I don't know what to do," she said. "I'm afraid. Wait, I get something."

She sat the boy on the floor. He howled in protest and wrapped his little body around one of his mother's legs. Alima murmured to him and stroked his head. He dropped his death grip on her leg and popped his thumb in his mouth and stared at Claire.

Claire made cooing sounds and smiled at him.

He crawled over to her, grabbed her pants leg and pulled himself up. He wobbled when he let go with one hand and held his arm up, begging to be picked up.

She picked him up, inhaling his sweet baby scent.

He made a grab for her earring, and she caught his hand and noisily kissed each of his fingers.

A vast yearning for a child swept through her, blindsiding her with its intensity.

Alima returned with a packet of papers tied with cotton twine. She took for Emir and handed Claire the papers.

Claire looked through them. She had given her their passports.

"Yemen is our home. I took Emir to the camps in Somalia." She reached over and tapped the papers. "See? Visas."

Claire checked the date. There was the problem. They expired in five months.

"Were you and Jerome married here in the states?"

"Yes." She nodded her head vigorously. "You said you could help us stay in the country."

Not exactly. Alima was assuming Claire could help with her visa problems because she worked for a law firm. Now, Claire felt on the hook to help her. The kid was so cute. "I know someone who might be able to help you. Give me your phone number." She handed Alima a business card.

Claire put Alima's number in her contacts. "Will you look at some pictures for me?"

Alima nodded.

Claire removed Jerome's picture, then spread the rest on the overturned milk crate. "Have you seen any of these people?"

Alima took her time looking at each photo, then she looked up at Claire and shook her head. She looked suspicious. "Will you still help us?"

"Yes, you'll be hearing from me." She gathered up the pictures and stuffed them in her bag. "Do you have someone who can stay with you?"

"Yes, there is a Yemeni community here."

Emir cried and fidgeted in her arms. "It's his sleep time."

Claire touched the boy's cheek. "You need to be strong for Emir," she told Alima.

Claire sat in the car thinking she just wasted valuable time and had taken on another job.

She made it to the office with only minutes to spare before her appointment with her boss.

He had his head down, reading briefs and popping Tums when she tapped on his door.

He motioned her to come in. "I have to read it in the paper that the police found a body at the truck stop and there's speculation it's connected to the Tutwiler case?" He raised one bushy brow. "Tell me you know what's going on."

She sat down and launched into her report. "The prints on the shells from both crime scenes are a match. The dead man is Jerome Matthews, a Big Pies driver, and he'd been stripped of his uniform. I think he delivered a pizza to Tutwiler's murderer and was killed for his clothes."

"Sounds like a pro hit, except Hawkins is still alive."

"I agree," Claire said, "But I can't find any dirt on Hawkins to implicate him. His bank records are clean."

"What about the rest of Tutwiler's staff?

"Rafe says there no evidence they're involved. I researched the last seven years of the Colorado Labor Board's records of complaints, and no one's filed a grievance against Tutwiler Industries. So, it doesn't look like it's an employee with a beef to settle."

"Someone went to a lot of trouble to kill him," Marsh said.

Claire agreed. "Remember Marvin Arden received a settlement? He plowed the settlement money into his company and expanded his business. I checked and Devlin's wife is barely making ends meet."

"We know a lot about who didn't kill him." Marsh folded his arms over his chest. "This is private information. Goes no further than you. Millennium had a sweetheart deal with Tutwiler. Backstrom's company got a kickback from Tutwiler for awarding contracts to

Tutwiler's steel company. When Tutwiler sold his steel company, he hurt Backstrom's bottom line. Then the news hit that Millennium Construction built the bridge and the slow grind to bankruptcy started. The Backstrom family name was trashed in the newspapers, and when Dave ran his car off a mountain pass, the papers rehashed the whole nasty business. Think Luke doesn't have an axe to grind?"

"He does, and his mother has the same motive he does."

"It's more believable that Luke hired a hitman than his mother." Marsh leaned back in his chair. "We're at thirty-six hours and counting since the murder, and Amanda is still the best suspect. Give me something I can use. If Amanda is charged, I need to create reasonable doubt in the jury's mind. Luke looks like the best candidate to make a jurist thing twice about convicting her." He put his glasses on and looked down at the papers he had been reading when she came in. "Keep in touch," he said dismissing her.

"One more thing," Claire said. "I need a favor. "Can you recommend a lawyer who does pro bono work for people who want their visas extended?"

Marsh sighed, exasperation thick in his voice. "You've found someone else to rescue. Claire, you can't save the world, but . . . oh hell. Talk to Jenny. She's got a list of pro bono legal clinics."

"Thank you." Claire headed to her office.

Marsh needed a suspect to sow discord with the DA and a jury. He hand-picked Luke for the job. She agreed Luke was the perfect man for the job, but she also knew all the things that could go wrong if she tried to prove up a case without solid evidence. And she didn't have any.

Her phone rang. Amanda.

"Everything okay?"

"I have a friend flying in and I'm on the way to the airport to pick them up. Want to meet us for drinks tonight?"

"Sure..."

"Meet us at The Grille at six-ish."

CHAPTER ELEVEN

CLAIRE SAT IN HER OFFICE EATING A SANDWICH AND A bag of chips from the vending machines. She was using her lunch break to mull over her Kirwin problem. She didn't want him living in her house unless she knew what happened in Chicago. His 'I made a mistake' confession was keeping her up nights teasing her with visions of all kinds of trouble turning up at her door.

She battled back and forth arguing with herself the pros and cons of calling Mac McNally for help. If she made the call, she might find out things about Kirwin best left buried—or other painful questions might be dredged up like the one she wrestled with before she fell asleep.

Is it forgivable to abandon a child?

Mac still worked as a PI for the Davis Law Firm, where she'd earned her chops before Marsh and Whitley came calling with bigger paychecks and better benefits.

She dialed his number.

But Mac wasn't answering. She left a voicemail.

As soon as she hung up, the phone rang. *Mac McNally.*

"Hey, that was quick," she said.

"You must need something," Mac said, "You're not the social type who calls to see how a guy is getting along."

"Sorry, Mac. How are you?"

"I'm fine and the Missus is, too. What's the problem?"

"Kirwin has turned up. He's living at my place." That sounded weak even to her.

"And Kirwin is?"

"Kirwin is the man who fathered me. You met his mother, Callie."

"Yeah." A pause. "Sorry to read about Callie dying, and sorry we didn't make it to her funeral, but we were thinking about you. So, the old boy showed up. I take it he needs something."

"He's in trouble with someone in Chicago. Do you have any contacts up there? I need to find out what's going on, but it has to be done quietly."

"I do have contacts—but hold on. Are you sure you want to get involved in this? I mean, what is he to you? You're a big girl now. You don't need a daddy, and you don't owe him anything. Could be trouble for you, Claire. You could just as well turn him out. He's done all right up to this point."

"Yeah, I know I could turn him out, but . . . I can't do it."

"Don't say I didn't warn you. Call Dan Alfonsi. He's a PI up there and he's good."

"Is he connected?"

"No more than you are. You want his number?"

"Yeah. But Mac, he better not be working with the mob."

"Claire, not everyone in Chicago is mobbed-up. Call the guy." Mac rattled off the numbers. "That's his cell.

He's always got his phone on him. Say my name first and he'll know I sent you. He's not cheap, but you won't be sorry you called him."

"Thanks, Mac. I appreciate it."

"Call me sometime when you want to get a cup a coffee."

"Oh, you know me. I'm terrible about keeping up with people."

"I'm no better than you are at it, but it doesn't mean me and the Missus don't care about you. Stay outta trouble." Mac hung up.

Claire got up and did something she should have done before she called Mac—close her office door.

She pondered the return on this deal. If she called Mac's contact and hired him, what was the worst that could happen? Kirwin got killed?

Oh, don't be such a drama queen.

She took a deep breath and dialed the Chicago PI who was no more mobbed up than she was.

"Dan Alfonsi."

"Mac McNally gave me your name. I'm Claire Callahan, a PI in Denver."

Alfonsi hung up and left her staring at her phone.

Well, at least Alfonsi knew how to contact her. And he knew she was connected to Mac. Maybe he and Mac weren't on such good terms.

Truck had texted while she was talking to Alfonsi. *"New info on Amanda. Call ASAP."*

From the background noise, Truck was in his car. She called him.

"Babe, we got us a new player. A boyfriend," he said.

"What?"

He laughed. "Your little heiress has a fuck buddy."

"She told me she was picking up a friend at the airport."

"Yassss, she sure did. They had themselves a hot and heavy reunion in the baggage area. I snapped a picture."

"You have a name yet?"

"Sure do. James Montgomery Allerton."

Claire was dumbstruck. The name James Allerton sounded familiar, but she couldn't quite place it.

"Oh, and Amanda's got wheels now, a new Tahoe from Hertz out at the airport."

"Okay," she said, pausing, trying to absorb it. "Thanks. I'll take it from here."

Claire put her phone down and rubbed her fingertips across her eyelids. One of her wild ideas bubbled up.

Did James Allerton target Amanda, then the two of them worked together to kill Tutwiler? Or did he kill her father to clear the way for him to get his hands on the Tutwiler money? Or was he just a man in love with a young woman?

Thinking anything could be true, Claire went to work searching the Net. What she found didn't put any of her wild theories to rest.

James was a native Bostonian, married to Elizabeth and father of one-year-old James Montgomery Allerton, junior.

Did Amanda know he was married?

Further digging turned up Allerton worked for a company who developed a staggering $5 billion dollars' worth of real estate on the East Coast.

She scrolled down and there was the name: Ingram & Mellor.

Ding, ding, ding. Luke Backstrom's partner on the Market project!

Was it possible Ingram & Mellor was trying to take over Millennium Construction and Amanda was caught in the fallout? Or was Amanda the target? Or maybe Millennium Construction *and* Amanda's holdings were both targets? If Ingram & Mellor took over Backstrom's construction company and Tutwiler Industries, they'd have a substantial footprint in Denver.

She did a name search on Elizabeth Allerton. Her maiden name was Ingram.

Wow. Daddy would fire James, and he would be lucky to see his kid on the holidays. Elizabeth had her own money, but she bet the wife would go after whatever James had.

Claire's head was spinning. Allerton was her worst nightmare. He held both Amanda's heart and her fortune in his hands.

No amount of kid glove handling was going to smooth over the news of James' marriage and his ties to the Backstrom family. Amanda's new-found self-confidence and poise would take a nosedive.

Claire applied pressure above her left eyebrow, to head off the headache that was coming. Marsh's reaction would be nuclear.

Claire sat back and closed her eyes, concentrating on herding her emotions into a box so she could focus on the facts. This rarely worked for more than five minutes at a time, but it was highly useful for the short period she could emotionally disconnect from the case.

Why would Allerton risk his marriage, his job, and the cushy lifestyle Elizabeth's money afforded?

Claire couldn't think of any reason unless his marriage to Elizabeth was ending and he was looking for a replacement with plenty of money.

Marsh was such a control freak. She dreaded telling him. He'd thought he had the Tutwiler fortune secure in the firm. Little did he know . . .

The last thing Claire wanted to do was talk to Marsh. But someone had to.

She buzzed Jenny to see if Marsh could squeeze her in. "It's very important," she said.

While she was waiting, Truck texted pictures of Amanda and Allerton wrapped around each other in the baggage area.

"He'll see you now," Jenny said.

With her phone in one hand and a file folder in the other, she knocked on Marsh's open door.

He frowned. "I don't need a jury consultant to read your face. Give me the bad news."

"When Amanda invited me for drinks tonight, she said she was picking a friend up at the airport." She handed him her phone. "That was taken a few minutes ago. His name is James Allerton. He's working with Luke Backstrom on The Market job."

Marsh sat back in his chair absorbing the blow.

"Allerton's married to the daughter of Mr. Ingram in Ingram and Mellor, the commercial real estate developer on the Market project," Claire said.

Marsh let out a low moan, then shook his head. "I suppose Allerton doesn't have a penny to his name?"

"I haven't turned him inside out, but it doesn't look like it." She picked up the phone and swiped through her pictures to the copies Truck had sent her of Allerton's birth certificate, marriage license, and the birth certificate of the child.

Marsh pulled at his lower lip as he looked at the documents. Then he sat back and said, "If Allerton is chasing after Amanda, it's because everything's turned to shit at home. Ingram probably had him sign a prenup so tight his asshole is still puckered. Allerton's on the prowl for a new woman with money."

Claire let him talk it through. Soon enough, he'd

work his way around to realizing his client and Allerton could be guilty of murder or targets of a hostile takeover.

"Allerton must be the reason Amanda's been pushing to get into the house," he said. "She hired a decorator last week. I've talked to her until I'm blue in the face. Until the estate is settled, she doesn't have the money to redecorate or buy the BMW she's picked out. She's a murder suspect and yet, all Amanda talks about is spending money. Good God, what a mess." He shook his head. "If this guy gets his hands on her money, she's up shit creek without a paddle."

"But she's broke right now. Maybe he'll leave."

"He wouldn't be here if he didn't have a reasonable certainty she'd inherit." Marsh slapped his front shirt pocket. Something he did when he was stressed and had forgotten he quit smoking. "Do you think they could have killed Tutwiler?"

Ah, Marsh had arrived at the point where she was. "I'll check it out, but probably not. I mean, how likely is that? Amanda doesn't have much money right now, and James doesn't seem to be the one with deep pockets at his house." She changed the subject. "Could the firm loan Amanda money to tide her over until she inherits?"

"Before you told me she was sleeping with a married man with no assets who is in cahoots with Backstrom, I would have thought about putting the firm's ass on the line for her. But not now. Folks like you are depending on me to keep their paychecks coming. I can't take that kind of risk."

He flicked his hand like he was waving away a pesky mosquito. "Damn it, this fuck-knuckle's bad news."

"Get him out of her life. He's probably telling her how much he loves her, and she's eating it up and going to hand over her fortune."

"I'm meeting them tonight for drinks."

Marsh jabbed his finger toward her. "Turn Allerton's life inside out. I want a lot of ammunition when I tell Amanda he's using her."

"She probably won't believe it, even if we have video and a written confession."

"It's my responsibility to tell her."

Claire nodded. "I'm on it."

She returned to her office to give it all a hard think.

The answer to *Who gains the most?* was always the same: *Amanda Tutwiler.*

But Claire couldn't believe the clueless fashionista was a stone-cold killer.

One thing Claire did know—when there's a gap between perception and reality, it's resolved in favor of reality. It would be a hard come-down for Amanda to find out Allerton loved her money more than her.

Her phone rang. *Blocked number.*

She hesitated before she answered. "Hello, Claire Callahan."

"Alfonsi, here. I'll take your case. Check your email for the contract. Look it over and sign it and we'll have a phone conference. *Capisce?*"

Capisce? Good God in Heaven. Not mobbed up, my ass.

"Sure. Thanks."

And the line went dead.

She opened her email, found his message, and attached was a contract for services. It looked like the boiler-plate contract Marsh gave to clients who used her services. She signed and returned it.

What would Dan Alfonsi, the Chicago PI who wasn't mobbed up, find out about Kirwin?

Claire arrived at the Grille early to scope out the scene from a booth in the back that faced the front door. She wanted to be able to watch the interaction between Amanda and James as they arrived.

She was drinking a glass of Riesling and people-watching when the couple finally arrived twenty minutes late. She didn't want to think about what they could have been doing that delayed them.

James was tall, had a good nose and jawline, and the haughty carriage of a man with a stick up his rear end.

Even from this distance, it was apparent Amanda was glowing with happiness. Her arm was tucked in the crook of Allerton's elbow.

Claire waved to catch their attention.

Amanda headed over and introduced him.

Claire stood and stuck out her hand. "Hi, I'm Claire Callahan, a friend of Amanda's."

"It's a pleasure to meet a friend of Amanda," James said.

"Claire's a PI. She works for Mr. Marsh, and she's my official keeper."

Claire sat on one side of the booth, they snuggled together across the table from her.

"Sorry we're late. James had to finish his workout. Poor baby, his job is so stressful." She laid her head on his shoulder, and he stroked her hair.

"The hotel has a lousy workout facility," James said. "Some of the cardio equipment didn't even work. I certainly hope there's a better gym near the house."

"Oh, there's a perfect place," Amanda said. "Lots of equipment, wet and dry saunas, indoor pool, even a yoga studio. You'll love it."

Claire thought James sounded like he was settling in for a long stay.

Their server arrived to take their drink orders. Claire

held up a hand indicating she was fine. Amanda ordered a glass of Pinot Grigio, and Allerton specified the 18-year-old vintage of Chivas.

Claire ordered appetizers for the table. Good thing she was able to expense the evening to the firm.

When the server left, Claire said, "I'm glad you took some time off to be with Amanda. It's been difficult for her."

Amanda gave Claire a sly smile. "James and I have been seeing each other for a while."

"Really?" Claire did her best to look surprised. "How did you meet?"

"At my bank in Boston. I was waiting to have some papers notarized for Mr. Marsh. James was waiting to see his broker, and we got to talking. We've been together ever since."

"Luckiest day of my life." James hugged Amanda.

"Nice story," Claire said as the drinks arrived. "How long will you be able to stay in Denver?"

"Denver is my new home. My firm is building here, the Market on Main project. You've heard of it?"

Claire nodded, and James kept talking.

"We usually don't bother ourselves with smaller projects. This is a first for the company, and they asked me to take it on as project manager. And of course, I'm thrilled to be here with Amanda and to look out for her interests."

By interests, Claire assumed he meant Amanda's inheritance.

"What company are you with?" Claire asked.

"I'm with Ingram and Mellor of Boston," he said. "We're real estate developers. Commercial projects only, quite large ones, actually."

Claire wanted to keep him talking. "Must be exciting work. Are you a lawyer?"

"No, no." He was shaking his head and smiling. "I am a hands-on guy. I like getting out in the field. The Market on Main is a multi-use commercial venture on a prime piece of downtown property. It's quite a coup, really, to have been selected to bring it to completion."

Claire kept her face neutral.

Amanda was beaming at James.

Claire bet she had no idea James was in business with Luke Backstrom, and nothing good was going to come from Luke nosing under Amanda's tent.

Big-eyed with pride, Amanda practically gushed: "We're getting married as soon as possible. I feel positively decadent sleeping with him. He's still married, but their divorce will be final in a few weeks."

James slipped his arm around Amanda's shoulders and looked at Claire. "My marriage has been over a long time. My wife and I decided to do the decent thing and allow each of us to have a chance at real happiness. Elizabeth hopes we have a wonderful life together."

Claire tried to keep from gagging. *What a load of bull.* No divorce had been filed.

"That's a very rare circumstance," Claire said. "Most divorces turn out to be long, epic battles over money and children."

A shadow crossed Allerton's face.

"Do you have a child?" Claire asked.

Amanda answered for him. "James has the most adorable little boy. He's going to live with his mother, he can come out and visit us when he's older. James and I will have our own babies.

How . . . thoughtful, Claire thought.

The server returned with crab cakes and artichoke dip.

When the server left the table, Claire said to Amanda, "Sounds like you've made a lot of plans."

"Yes." Amanda looked smug. "Now you know why I'm not returning to Boston. I feel so grown up. I've never done anything like this in my life."

James picked up his glass and held it up. "A toast to us?"

A starry-eyed Amanda clicked her wine glass to his and said, "To us."

When they'd finished toasting each other, Claire asked James, "Will your firm be offering you other projects in Denver?"

He wiped dip from the corners of his mouth. "They don't know it, but I plan to see The Market to completion and then strike out on my own. Just look at the skyline downtown. Everywhere you look, you see building cranes. Legal pot has brought a ton of new money to this town. I intend to get my share."

"James is so smart," Amanda cooed. "They'll hate to lose him in Boston, but he thinks he needs a fresh start."

He pulled Amanda closer to him and told her, "I promise you I'll make you the happiest woman alive."

Amanda was still basking in her happy groove when she confided to Claire, "We're going ring shopping. I saw the perfect ring when we were at Cherry Creek."

"You should have shown it to me," she said.

"We weren't ready to announce our engagement," Amanda said with a sly smile.

"Have you thought about having a long engagement?" Claire asked. "Give yourselves time to put down some roots and get your house fixed like you want it? Nothing lovelier than a June wedding."

James answered for her. "We want to be together as soon as possible."

"James loves me unconditionally," Amanda said. You know I've never had that. It's a little fast, he's still married, I get all that. But when it's right, you just know it. And James and I are perfect for each other."

"Couldn't have said it better, darling." He leaned over and kissed her on the lips.

Then he said to Claire, "Now, when is all this police business going to be over. Amanda has been through the wringer long enough. It's your job to clear her good name."

Claire resisted asking when 'Tutwiler' was a good name around Denver.

"James, it's not like you see on television. I can't give you a time and a date. Investigations are on a schedule of their own making. Everything that can be done is being done. No one's dragging their heels, and I realize how difficult this is for Amanda."

Claire signaled for the check.

"I simply want what's best for Amanda," James said. "I'm sure you understand that. She's depends on me. Her good name has to be restored before I can sell her father's businesses and reinvest the money."

Claire looked at Amanda. "Is that what you want?"

"Absolutely, James has a brilliant head for business."

Claire wasn't going to ask how Amanda knew that. "Perhaps you should meet with a professional money manager. The firm can give you some recommendations."

"Amanda is lucky to have a man of my caliber and experience to look after her." James had his back up. "My advice won't cost her a penny, and you know a money manager will charge her a hefty fee."

What a poser.

He was selling Amanda a bill of goods before the bright white band of skin on his wedding ring finger had time to pick up a tan.

"You're going to run out of here and tattle to Mr.

Marsh," Amanda said. "It won't work. I'm an adult and James and I have made our plans."

Claire offered a polite smile. "I wish you both the best."

She paid the bill and left the Grille, itching to pull out her phone, but waited, not wanting them to come out and catch her in the act of tattling to Marsh.

She drove a couple of blocks and then called Marsh.

He answered on the first ring. "Well? What do you think of Allerton?"

"He's in charge. He's blowing warm air up her skirt, telling her a quick divorce is in the offing, so they can marry."

"Not good news, but about what I expected you to tell me. Do you think Amanda knows of Allerton and Backstrom are in cahoots?"

"I don't think so. All she's thinking about is ring shopping and wedding planning. Allerton plans to leave Boston to start his own company here. Guess where he's going to get the start-up money?"

"Not on a bet. I'll talk some sense into Amanda."

"I don't know how you'll pry her away from Allerton."

Marsh chuckled. "I do. You're going to create a diversion."

On that note, Marsh hung up, leaving her to figure out how to separate Allerton and Amanda long enough for Marsh to break the bad news.

CHAPTER TWELVE

IT WASN'T QUITE DAWN WHEN CLAIRE TIPTOED OUT THE door without waking Kirwin. She was getting good at it.

On the way to work, she fine-tuned her plan to throw a monkey wrench into Allerton's day.

The two-hour time difference between Denver and the East Coast meant it would be past 9 AM in Boston by the time she reached the office. Time to launch a bombshell that would keep Allerton too busy to accompany Amanda to a meeting with Marsh.

Except for two junior lawyers who looked like they'd pulled an all-nighter, she had the office to herself.

She sat her bag on her desk and opened the blinds. The Rockies stood in relief in a cerulean sky. The weatherman had promised a perfect autumn day, cloudless, bright sunshine and crisp fall temperatures. If she wasn't consumed with the Tutwiler case, she'd drive up into the high country to see the aspens turning and the elk coming down to the meadows.

Instead, she booted up her computer, surfed to the Ingram and Mellor website and found their phone number. She jotted it down.

Now she needed his home number. She pulled up AnyWho.com. With either a name or a phone number, she could find an address.

Several James Allertons were listed with Boston addresses and phone numbers, but only one James Montgomery Allerton was listed.

Her first call was to the company.

A woman answered. "Ingram and Mellor."

"Perhaps you can help me," Claire said. "I'm Gwen, Luke Backstrom's secretary. Mr. Allerton is here in Denver working on The Market project with my boss. He has a couple of questions for Mr. Ingram before his meeting this morning with Mr. Allerton."

There was a long pause, and then the woman cautiously answered. "I'm afraid there's some mistake. Mr. Allerton is working in Baltimore."

Claire pushed her point saying, "No, I met Mr. Allerton yesterday and Mr. Backstrom needs a few minutes of Mr. Ingram's time."

"Mr. Ingram is not in the office, but I'll let him know."

"Thanks," Claire said. "It'll all grind to a halt here if we don't hear from him today."

If his office thought Allerton was in Baltimore, probably his family did, too.

Next, Claire called the Allerton's home. A young girl answered, and when Claire asked to speak to Mr. Allerton, the child said, "Daddy's in Baltimore."

"Could I speak to your mom?" Claire asked.

"Okay."

It took a couple of minutes for Mrs. Allerton to pick up, and when she did, she sounded wary. She asked Claire who she was and how she had gotten their home number.

"I'm a private investigator with the Marsh and

Whitley law firm in Denver. You can check if you like." She gave Mrs. Allerton the firm's number and website. "If you're interested in discussing your husband's activities in Denver, please call and I'll fill you in."

Then she hung up.

Within five minutes, Claire's office phone rang.

"Claire Callahan," she answered.

"Ms. Callahan, this is Elizabeth Allerton. You wanted to talk."

"Yes, thank you for the callback. I am acting on behalf of Charles Marsh, the senior partner in the firm. He represents a young woman whose father was recently murdered."

"I don't see that has anything to do with my husband."

"Mr. Allerton is in Denver claiming he is the project supervisor for an Ingram and Mellor project. He's living with our client, a highly vulnerable young woman who is grieving her father."

"You've made a mistake," Ms. Allerton said. "James is in Baltimore. You can verify that with the company."

"I have spoken with the company. Mr. Allerton isn't in Baltimore. He's here and he has asked our client to marry him."

There was silence for several seconds. Then: "Why are you doing this to me?"

"I'm not doing anything to you. I'm protecting our client. I've emailed you a time and date-stamped picture of my client and your husband in front of the Marriott in downtown Denver. I'm sorry for the pain this causes you. By now, Ingram and Mellor have had time to call the Baltimore project site and verify your husband isn't there."

"Then why are you telling me all this?" Now the voice was angry. "Do you want me to fly out to Denver and bitch-slap this girl and take back my man? I know what kind of man he is, and here's a tidbit you can share with his fiancée. James owns a laptop and his clothes. Nothing else. Even the car he drives is provided by the firm. His clothes and computer are all he'll walk away from this family with, and if after knowing that, this woman is still enamored with him enough to marry him, then they deserve each other. I hope they're miserable."

And with that, she hung up.

Elizabeth Allerton was in full-blown angry-as-hell scorned woman mode.

Claire searched online for a pay phone to make her next call. There weren't many left, but by typing her zip code into the PayPhoneDirectory.com web site, she found the one closest to her.

She told Jenny she was ducking out for an hour and would be on her cell.

The pay phone was located on a corner six blocks away in front of a Mom and Pop store selling breakfast burritos and piñatas.

Claire hadn't heard the satisfying clatter of coins dropped into a pay phone in years. Once she had a dial tone, she called the Occupational Safety and Health Administration's anonymous tip line.

She reported Millennium Construction was in violation of OSHA safety regulations at the Market on Main construction site in Denver. She left a detailed message about scaffolding doubling for ladders, no guard rails or toe boards in place to protect workers on platforms, no safety harnesses and tether lines provided for the guys working up high, and no respirators for workers cutting through old concrete.

She hung up, satisfied with her work. The diversion was launched, and it would be fun to watch it unfold.

She bet James had already gotten an earful from his outraged father-in-law and wife.

OSHA inspectors might not get to the building site today, but when they did, they'd shut construction down and spend days, even weeks investigating.

She drove back to her office to indulge in some thinking time. Once at her desk, she wrote the names James Allerton, Luke Backstrom, and Amanda Tutwiler on a legal pad and then, drew arrows connecting the names in a circle.

What did each of them know about the others? Did Luke know Allerton was Amanda's fiancé or did Allerton know the Backstroms' history with the Tutwilers?

She had no idea, and when a case hit a wall, the only thing to do is rattle cages, kick down doors, and ask more questions.

Claire had the nagging feeling, not a thought, but a gut emotion, she was missing something in this case. Some big unknown, something that would be totally unexpected because she didn't even know to look for it.

She needed to war-game her strategy—imagine she failed to solve the case, then work back through the steps that brought her to where she was.

Maybe she could find the elusive piece she was searching for. Doing this premortem would correct her natural bias of believing in her own genius. She'd have to act as her devil's advocate.

Claire had been holding tightly to her belief Amanda wasn't capable of hiring a hit man. She'd taken her alibi had face value and dubbed her a vacuous fashionista, but Claire hadn't seen her in over a year. What if she was reading the cues wrong?

She looked through her notes until she found the name of the professor whose class Amanda claimed she was attending the night of the murder. She called Boston College, was connected to his office, and identified herself.

"Yes, how may I help you?" he said.

"Professor Kotterna, I'm investigating the murder of the father of Amanda Tutwiler, a student of yours."

"I've told the police all I know. She was in my class the evening in question," he said quickly.

"I know. I was hoping you would share your impressions of the girl."

There was a long pause during which Claire wondered if the connection was severed.

"This was the third class she took from me," Professor Kotterna said. "I teach Western Civilization. My classes are seminars. There're only ten to twelve students in each section, the classes are kept small to encourage students to discuss the readings. Ms. Tutwiler didn't participate in the class discussion, and she seemed somehow . . . removed from the setting. She didn't engage in the usual student chatter before class and she always left the class alone. She passed the two prior classes, but she is an unremarkable student. Her writing demonstrates she'd done the readings, but her papers lack the depth of analysis I expect at this level." He then paused before adding, "The young woman has no charisma, no gumption. She's a blank canvas, and she's not looking for a paintbrush."

Immediately he tried to walk back his last statement: "I shouldn't have said that. I should have spoken only about her class performance. She's lost her father, and I don't want to make trouble for her."

"Nothing you have said will be repeated," Claire said. I was perception-checking my own view of her and I appreciate you speaking openly with me."

"Will she be coming back to class? If not, she should withdraw with the registrar's office."

"I'll pass that along to Amanda. Thank you for your time."

After considering the conversation with Kotterna, Claire questioned her assumption Amanda showed initiative when she left Denver for Boston. What if she was only fleeing the horrors in Denver to the only other city where she had a connection? The city where her mother had attended college.

Professor Kotterna's description of Amanda was spot-on to Claire's, and not far off the mark from what Hawkins Reynolds had said about her.

A girl with no passion wasn't likely to hire a killer and send him on a cross-country trip to murder her father. But a passive girl could be persuaded to follow someone else's lead.

Claire checked the time. She preferred questioning Amanda face-to-face, but Marsh's upcoming meeting made that impossible. Once he outed her fiancé as a lying gold-digger, fat chance Amanda would talk to Claire.

Claire called Amanda and asked for a few minutes of her time.

The girl sounded petulant.

"I'll keep this short," Claire promised. "I'd rather we talked in person, but we don't have time."

"I'm seeing you soon. Can't it wait?"

"No, you're meeting with your Mr. Marsh about the estate. I need to talk to you about you and your dad. Just a few minutes, please." Claire barreled ahead without waiting for a reply. "You and your dad were all the family either of you had. You lived together until you moved to Boston, and you may know more than you realize about who would want to hurt him."

"I haven't seen him or talked to him in over a year."

"But you lived with him for twenty years. Was he afraid? Did he mention anyone he was worried about?"

"He was mad. All the time, hopping mad, and I tried to stay out of his way."

"He kept guns in the house. Did he carry? Or did Hawkins carry?"

"Hawkins might know. I don't."

"Were he and Hawkins hypervigilant about safety in the car and around the house?"

"I didn't pay attention. The house has a good alarm system. You don't understand. Dad and I never talked—he just ordered me around. He would come home from work and close himself in his study. I hid out upstairs in my room. Lots of times he ate dinner in the office, and I ate in the kitchen with Hawkins and Martha."

"Tell me about Hawkins. Were he and your dad ever on the outs?"

"No, Hawkins was the glue that held us all together after Mom died."

"Never any friction between them?"

"No. Go see him. He was more than a driver to Dad."

Claire took another course of questioning. "Do you know Luke Backstrom?"

"Not really. I knew who he was when I saw him in court. I went to an all-girls prep school, and he's a couple of years older than me. Our paths never crossed except at the trial."

"Was he ever at your house?"

"I never saw him there."

"Did you ever meet his mother, Sonja?"

"Why are you asking me all this stuff?"

"Remember James told me my job was to clear your name? I'm doing my job."

"Okay, but this is boring. Sonja and Mom worked on charity events together and she came by the house a couple of times, but that was years ago. I never saw her again until the trial."

"Did you ever hear Sonja and your mom argue?"

"What would they have to argue about? Claire this is stupid."

If Amanda didn't know her mother and Dave Backstrom had a lengthy affair, Claire didn't want to be the one to tell her.

"Do you think either of the Backstroms had your father killed?"

"I don't know!" She was annoyed. "How would I know? How many times do I have to tell you? I don't know anything."

"Who was the first person you thought of when Mr. Marsh told you your dad was dead?"

"No one. I . . . uh . . . I was relieved. I didn't think about who might have done it."

"Give me one reason to convince me you weren't involved."

The silence stretched out. Claire could hear Amanda breathing.

"I don't know how to do something like that. Like, do people Google up a killer? Or know friends who off people?"

Claire read the suspects' names. "Who's missing from this list?"

"How would I know? Isn't that what you're paid for?"

Claire realized she'd pushed her as far as she could. She laid her phone down thinking she had no evidence Amanda hired a killer, but she couldn't prove she didn't.

And Marsh wasn't going to be happy. He didn't want a whiff of suspicion associated with his client.

Claire sat across from Marsh in one of his comfy leather chairs while they waited for Amanda to arrive at the office.

"Here's how I'm going to approach Amanda," he said. "Elizabeth Allerton has filed for divorce. I'll hand her a copy of the petition. The date it was filed is right on top of it. Then I'll explain to her that a divorce with child custody arrangements to be agreed upon can take as long as fourteen months to finalize in Massachusetts." He shrugged. "We'll pick up the pieces and help her move forward. I assume we are not expecting Mr. Allerton to join us?"

Claire smiled. "I believe he's busy with something else."

Marsh held up one hand. "Don't tell me. I want plausible deniability."

Jenny knocked on Marsh's door and announced Amanda had arrived.

"Send her in," Marsh told her.

A few moments later, Amanda strode in looking unhappy and distracted. She wore all black, cashmere sweater, and skinny jeans tucked into the tops of her boots. The only hint of color was a red scarf wound around her neck.

She sat in the chair by Claire. "James will be here as soon as he can. Something is haywire on the construction site, and he had to go over there."

Amanda's six-carat blue topaz ring surrounded with diamonds caught the light as she moved her hands. She caught Claire looking, and held out her left hand. "You like?"

"It's beautiful."

"I put in on my credit card. James has all his money tied up in a deal."

Marsh gulped and then managed to congratulate her on her engagement. "Thank you for taking the time to meet this morning. Too bad James is running late, but we just have a few things to talk about."

Marsh folded his arms over his chest. "Did you know James is supposed to be working in Baltimore this week? Both his firm and his family thought he was there."

She looked confused, then angry. "How would you know?" Recognition dawned. She shot a look at Claire. "You've been snooping. How could you? And what business is it of yours anyway?" She jumped up.

"If you could give me just a moment," Marsh said. "I'm your attorney, and I'm responsible for keeping you informed so you may make the best decisions. Please." He gestured at her chair. "Let's talk about this." He placed the Allerton divorce petition on the desk facing Amanda.

She leaned closer to his desk and glanced at them. "What? I know all this. They're getting divorced."

Marsh explained. "Look at the date the petition was filed. It was just filed. With decisions to be made for the child's support and custody, the Allerton divorce might not be granted for over a year."

She was shaken, but game. "So? We'll live together. It's not the nineteenth century."

"Indeed, it isn't. Back then, a man asked a woman to marry him with the intent of supporting her and he bought his bride's ring."

"I don't have to listen to this," Amanda said half standing.

"Please sit down. It's to your advantage to listen. Allerton's wife brought the bulk of the assets into the marriage and since it was her premarital property, she gets to keep it in the divorce. James is coming to you penniless. Do you want to support him?"

Amanda leaned forward like she was going to answer.

Marsh kept talking. "The family court will take a dim view of James abandoning his son and moving across the country to live with you during the couple's separation. This divorce will not be resolved quickly and may not be resolved in a way that is in the best interests of Allerton or his son. If you marry him, you will always have Elizabeth in your life. She's the mother of his child. It's in your interest to let this divorce unfold with you as a bystander for several reasons. You're risking your financial future on a man who let you buy your engagement ring. He's lied to you about the timing of his divorce, and I doubt he's told you the truth about the state of his financial affairs."

Claire touched Amanda's arm. "You deserve a lot better than him. He cheated with you. Who's to say he won't cheat on you?"

Marsh picked up the ball and was telling Amanda they would weather this storm with her when the office door burst open. James Allerton hurried in with Jenny hard on his heels.

"I'm sorry sir, he didn't give me a chance to let you know he was here," Jenny said.

Amanda half-stood as though she were going to run to James, then looked uncertain and sank back in her chair.

Marsh stood, offering his hand to James. "I'm —"

"I know who you are," James said.

"Please, have a seat. Glad you could make it."

Allerton ignored him and bent down in front of Amanda. He took her hands in his. "Listen to me, sweet girl."

Amanda lifted her head to him.

"I don't know what's going on here, but I suspect they're filling your head with lies about me," James said. "I love you. You're wearing my ring. Whatever they've said to you, nothing has changed the feelings we have for each other."

Amanda laced her fingers with his.

"After you left Boston, I couldn't quit thinking of you, of how much I wanted to be with you." He brushed a kiss on her cheek. "I came here to start a new life with you."

He stroked her hair. "No one will ever love you as much as I do. Stay the course with me, darling, we'll have a wonderful life." He pulled her to her feet and into his arms. Over the top of her head, James was smiling at Marsh.

They stepped apart and held hands. Amanda shot an angry look at Marsh and Claire. "I don't know if I can ever forgive either of you."

Marsh stood, resting his fingertips on this desk. "Mr. Allerton, how long have you known Luke Backstrom?"

Allerton looked puzzled. "I don't know why that's any of your business, but I have nothing to hide. I've recently started working with him on a deal.

Claire's liar-liar pants-on-fire meter didn't budge off zero.

"Perhaps," Marsh said, "you should ask Amanda about the history of the Backstroms and Tutwilers." He turned to Amanda, and his voice became gentle. "Get to know him better. Have a long engagement. The man a woman marries is the biggest influence in her life."

Amanda was defiant and furious. "Leave us alone! Stay out of our lives. Just probate the estate. Do you hear me?" She pointed at Marsh. "But you owe me. You have connections and you're going to help James get his business going. Kicking a couple doors open for him is the least you can do after what you've done."

She swung around and faced Claire. "How dare you go behind my back and snoop?"

She grabbed James's hand and pulled him to the door. Amanda paused and turned back to look at Marsh and Claire. "I mean it. Get my money out of probate."

They stalked out into the hallway.

Claire closed the door behind them.

Marsh shrugged. "I don't want to lose the Tutwiler business, but the firm will survive. We'll pick up new clients, and maybe they won't require as much hand-holding as Amanda. I've offered her sound advice. It's her choice to take it or leave it." He pointed at Claire. "Until she formally severs the client relationship, we still work for her. Which means you need to get out there and clear her name."

Marsh looked down at his watch.

"I'm due in court in half an hour. I wouldn't mind if you called Amanda and tried to soothe her ruffled feathers. A bird in the hand is better than two in the bush. It takes time and money to drum up new clients."

Right. I get the crap job.

"I'll do my best," Claire said before she left. Though she was thinking, James was soothing Amanda's ruffled feathers and putting the kibosh on Amanda having anything more to do with her.

Claire needed lard and sugar. She headed for the Eighteenth Street Bakery for a quiet lunch by herself.

CHAPTER THIRTEEN

CLAIRE SAT BY THE WINDOW IN THE EIGHTEENTH STREET Bakery dining on her favorite sandwich, a bacon panini with melted jack cheese. She had her eye on a big cinnamon roll.

She hoped some of the things she and Marsh said to Amanda would take root. If Amanda could be a teeny bit objective about Allerton, she could grab her fortune and make a run for it.

Women fall too hard, too fast for the line: *No one will ever love you as much as I do.* It's irresistible. James was pressuring her to believe he's the best she'd ever have, and she'd better snap up the offer while it was still available.

Claire checked her texts on the way to the car. Rafe had let her know that Hawkins had been released from the hospital. She headed to Tutwiler's house.

Claire was curious how Hawkins saw his job changing now that his boss was dead. He would no longer be needed to drive Tutwiler, and Allerton and Amanda were tooling around Denver in their rental, waiting to buy the Beemer she had her eye on. No doubt it would have fur seats and gold-plated radio knobs.

She pulled through Tutwiler's circle drive and parked near the garage. Hawkins lived upstairs.

The garage doors were open, and four expensive-looking cars were parked inside. There was the black four-door Mercedes Hawkins had driven Tutwiler in and three others that Claire decided needed a closer look.

She would never have guessed Tutwiler was a muscle car collector. They looked like he had driven them off the showroom floor and parked them here. Not a speck of dust. On the wall of the garage in front of each car was a sign with the make and model, as if this was a museum. His collection looked valuable like everything in the house.

She took the outside staircase up to a small covered porch and Hawkins' front door.

He answered the bell dressed in gray sweatpants and a white long sleeve shirt. His arm was still in a sling.

"Oh hi. If I'd known you were coming, I would have put on a pot of coffee. Come in."

"Thanks, I just wanted to see how you are doing."

The living room overlooked the Tutwiler gardens. There was a small balcony with two chairs and a table between them. When the gardens were in bloom, it would be a peaceful spot to read a book.

The apartment was open style, the living room flowing into a galley kitchen and a small eating area. A short hallway off the living area looked like it led to the bedroom.

He offered her the sofa and he took a chair, resting his elbow on the arm, taking some of the weight off the sling around his neck.

"How are you feeling?"

"Lucky," he said, rearranging the sling so his arm was more comfortable. "I'm going to recover full use of my arm." He looked up at Claire. "I still feel like hell he died, but I have a second chance, working for Amanda. I'm not going to let anything happen to her."

"She's happy you're staying on. Are you up for a few questions?"

He nodded. "Fire away."

"You probably knew Mr. Tutwiler as well as anyone," Claire said. "What was his state of mind the last few days before the shooting?"

"I've been over and over that in my mind. Things were normal. He was working on finding new vendors for barware for the brew pubs. He didn't seem anxious or worried."

"Was he angry?"

"He was an angry person. Anger is—was, his natural state. But he didn't seem fearful about anything. We took the usual precautions and varied our route. But those are the kind of precautions we have been taking for over a year."

"Did he receive any phone calls that upset him?"

Hawkins shook his head. "Not that I know of and I overheard his side of all the phone calls he took in the car."

"What about confrontations? Anyone shake a fist as you drove by or yell at him?"

"No, thank God. That all ended last year." Hawkins eased his elbow off the arm of the chair and cupped his hurt arm with his good hand.

"Any ideas about who killed him?"

"That's all I've thought about," Hawkins said. "I think the killer is connected to last year's crisis. Mr. Tutwiler has been hunkered down, keeping a low profile. He was building up his existing businesses. He wasn't in the middle of a hostile takeover; he wasn't trying to buy a piece of land out from under someone." Hawkins gave a one-shoulder shrug. "That's my opinion based on what I overheard in the car and how he seemed after taking a meeting."

"What was the relationship between the Backstroms and the Tutwilers before the bridge collapsed?"

"Sonja was a friend of Mrs. Tutwiler. Now that was a long time ago, and Mrs. Tutwiler's been dead going on six years. Of course, back then no one could imagine what horrible things would happen," Hawkins said. "The women worked together on some charities, and I remember them chatting on the back terrace and drinking wine, just as happy as can be."

"All this was happening before Lucy had her affair with Sonja's husband?"

He looked uncomfortable. "'I didn't know you knew. The affair and the women's friendship were going on at the same time. I don't know if the two women drifted apart or if Mrs. Backstrom found out about Lucy and her husband and quit coming around. There were certainly no shouting matches on the back terrace."

"Sonja Backstrom had to have been humiliated," Claire said. "Maybe she cleaned house and had Tutwiler killed so all three of them would be out of her life. Both the Tutwilers hurt her badly."

Hawkins was shaking his head. "I can't see her doing that. It's just my opinion, but she struck me as an airhead socialite. She and Lucy could plan a charity gala that knocked everyone's socks off, but I don't think she would come down from her pedestal to deal with the kind of people you have to negotiate with to hire a killer. I just can't see it."

"What about Luke?"

"I don't know him." Hawkins said. "I was never

around him. He never came to the house, at least while I was here, and I never saw him talking with Mr. Tutwiler. I know he has taken over the company since Dave killed himself. I don't know how that's going."

"Luke has two projects under construction. The Market on Main and a condominium going up in the central part of town. Do you know who the real estate developer is on the Market project?"

"No, since he sold the steel company, Mr. Tutwiler hasn't been involved in any construction projects."

"Luke's working with Ingram and Mellor out of Boston. Their man on the job out here is James Allerton.

Hawkins' jaw dropped slightly. "Amanda's fiancé? Does she know?"

"Mr. Marsh told her this morning. Didn't faze her. She and James walked out the door hand in hand."

"My God, do you think Luke Backstrom killed Mr. Tutwiler and is plotting a takeover of Tutwiler Industries? He could be using this Allerton guy to romance Amanda."

"I've been down that road, too," Claire admitted. "I don't have any evidence that James' and Luke's business together isn't on the up and up."

"You can't let this happen to Amanda. She admires you. Talk to her. She's too old to be as naïve as she is, but her father never let her make a decision and fall on her face when the stakes were small, and now, she's floundering."

"I know, I'll try, but she's angry at me for snooping, and Allerton is telling her what she desperately wants to hear: 'I love you.' At least we have some time. The estate is nowhere near being settled."

Hawkins looked hurt Amanda had shut him out. "I met James yesterday when Amanda came by to show me her ring. She didn't tell me anything about James. What do you know about him?"

"He's married and has a child."

Hawkins looked horrified. "You have to run him off."

"I can't do that," Claire said, "but we have one thing working for us. Marsh says it could be a year before his divorce is granted. That doesn't mean Allerton won't have his hand in the till as soon as Amanda inherits, but at least they won't be married."

"She hasn't had much happiness in her life, and I'm not going to let him hurt her."

"I hope she listens to you." Claire stood to leave. "Thanks for seeing me. I've tired you. Don't get up. I'll let myself out."

As she drove to her office, she mulled over her visit with Hawkins. As Tutwiler's right-hand man, he had insights no one else could offer, but she hadn't learned anything she didn't already know. She felt like Pokey Butt, the hamster she had as a kid, going around and around on the exercise wheel.

She was taking the exit on to the interstate when her phone vibrated.

Rafe texted: *Can u talk?*

She called him. "Hey, what's up?

He sounded bone tired. "We found the Big Pies car in the old Barnard Moving Company warehouse. On North Broadway, right where you guessed it would be. The killer hid it back in a corner behind an old forklift. If we hadn't been searching every one of those warehouses on foot, we'd never have seen it."

Smart, Claire thought.

"The fingerprints from the car match the prints we took at Tutwiler's, and we got DNA. off a piece of half-eaten pizza. We still need a name for our suspect."

"How long until you get the DNA results?"

"It was a real pissing match, but we got approved to use the Biologics lab. They can get us a quicker turnaround than the state lab. The only reason Beekman caved is he's hoping to get off the front page of the newspaper."

"Let's hope his DNA is on file, even though his fingerprints aren't."

"Keep your fingers crossed. We still need the damn gun. The DA loves to have the prints on the murder weapon when he goes to court."

Claire was thinking out loud. "I think you can kiss off finding the gun. It's sprouted wings and flown away, and nothing else about this case makes sense. We have DNA and fingerprints and a witness. No pro shot Tutwiler, and Hawkins would have recognized our suspects. Yet, I have no evidence any of them hired a hit."

"Little frustrated, are we?"

"You bet, I'm crazy." She hesitated. "Maybe, Tutwiler's killer knows he's not in any database."

"I'll play along." Rafe sounded sarcastic. "How do we find him?"

Claire backpedaled in the face of his annoyance. "It's only a theory I'm working on."

Rafe's voice was now loaded with irritation. "Dammit, we have four, maybe five people who are good for putting a hit on Tutwiler. It's one of them."

"Rafe . . ."

"Sorry, didn't mean to snap," he said. "We aren't close to making an arrest, and that damn Lancaster woman is like a terrier with a bone. Even if she has nothing new to report, she's on the front page accusing the cops of being incompetent."

"I'm sorry, let's move on. Got a minute for a question?"

"Make it short."

"Was there anything unusual about Dave Backstrom's suicide last year?"

"No. Not a thing. His tox screen was clean. Crash scene investigators said it looked like he deliberately drove off the pass. Why?"

"Dave's death cleared the way for Luke to run the family business."

"There's no indication it was anything but a straightforward suicide," Rafe said. "What does Backstrom's suicide have to do with Tutwiler's murder? I can't be chasing ghosts when I got plenty of suspects in my face."

"When was the last time you slept?"

He didn't answer her question. Instead he said, "Beekman's ordered me to see the psych. He thinks my personal life is impinging on my work life. Impinging. That's his word. I have a court date. I'm going to have to plead with some judge that I should be able to raise my own daughter."

"I'm sorry. How is she doing?"

"Not good. She loves her grandparents and she doesn't understand why they'd put her through this. Look, I gotta go."

"Sure. Tell Lily I said hi."

CLAIRE HAD NEVER MET Sonja Backstrom. All the information she had of her was second-hand. As she exited the freeway and neared the Backstrom's family home, she ran a couple of interview scenarios through her head.

Should she start focused and lob a zinger, like *Did you kill Tutwiler?* Or go wide and establish rapport, expressing sympathy for the loss of her husband before hitting her with the tough questions?

She wanted to crack Sonja's perfect poise and rattle her until something interesting shook loose.

She decided to go with softening Sonja up before she asked the tough questions. A slow start would give her time to study Sonja's body language and her tone of voice.

She pulled into the drive of the Backstrom home. Most likely built in the 1950s, the house was a long one-story beige brick rectangle with windows marching below the roof line. The two flat planes of the roof met in a low peak at the midpoint of the house, broken by a wide chimney.

Claire knocked on the front door hoping Luke wouldn't answer. A woman holding a feather duster opened the door, and Claire asked to see Mrs. Backstrom. She was directed to the living room to wait.

The room was elegant and understated with hardwood floors and a large leather sofa with a coffee table the size of Claire's breakfast table. In front of the fireplace, two overstuffed chairs faced each other, separated by a small table.

A dishwater blonde, thick with middle age, walked into the room, wearing slouchy sweat pants and an oversized shirt. Not at all what Claire expected.

"I'm Sonja Backstrom. How can I help you?"

Before Claire could answer, there was recognition in Sonja's eyes.

"You're that investigator with Marsh and Whitley."

"I'm Claire Callahan. I'm investigating Morgan Tutwiler's murder."

"You're wasting your time. Talk to his daughter."

Claire smiled. *Wow, she is not happy to see me.* "I won't take much of your time. I just have a few questions."

Sonja flicked her hand toward the chairs around the fireplace. "Please, have a seat."

Claire sat across from her. "I was sorry to hear of your husband's death. I know that must be hard for you and for Luke. He has the burden of running the company while he grieves."

Sonja slumped in her chair. "I miss Dave every day."

"I haven't suffered a loss like yours," Claire said, "but I can see how painful it is."

Sonja pulled a tissue out of the box on the table and wiped her eyes. Claire noticed she'd bitten her nails to the quick. "You didn't come to talk about my Dave. I don't know anything about Morgan Tutwiler's murder, but he got what he deserved."

Claire nodded. "He didn't make your life easy, did he?"

"Morgan Tutwiler as good as drove my husband's car off Miner's Pass. You have no idea how bad it was. The trial, then our business dried up, and the press dragged Dave's name through the mud. My Dave was in so much pain, he couldn't stand it anymore."

"I'm sorry. I'm sure Luke found it hard to watch his father suffer."

"Of course, he did. Luke came back after graduation just in time to see us lose everything we worked for." She dabbed her eyes and blew her nose. "You don't really care about what we've been through. What do you want?"

Claire pulled out her phone and scrolled to a picture of James. "Do you recognize this man?"

Sonja took the phone and studied the picture, then handed it back, "No I don't think I've ever seen him. Who is he?"

"He's James Allerton. He's working with Luke on the Market project."

"That's turned into such a mess. OSHA shut the site down, and the crews have taken other jobs. You can't blame them, but this whole mess is going to ruin Luke."

"I hope Luke has the Market up and running soon. You two need to catch a break." Claire held her phone out for Sonja to look at a second picture, one of James and Amanda. "James is Amanda Tutwiler's fiancé."

Sonja recoiled. First confusion crossed her face, then anger. "You're lying. You people would do anything to hurt us. Luke would never involve himself with anyone in the Tutwiler family."

"Maybe Luke doesn't know about James' connection to the Tutwilers. Do you think that Amanda and Allerton are planning a hostile take-over of Millennium Construction?"

"No." She was vehement. "It's all lies."

"The Tutwilers were always a problem, weren't they? Dave and Lucy canoodling behind your back, and then Tutwiler throwing Dave under the bus when the bridge collapsed."

"You hateful bitch. Coming in here and talking to me like this." She shot to her feet. "Get out."

Claire walked to the front door. "Did you kill Tutwiler?"

Sonja was close behind her. "Get out, get out of my house!"

"Or did you get Luke to kill Tutwiler for you?" Claire said.

Sonja screamed and put her hands over her ears. "Leave us alone."

Claire opened the door. "I'll let myself out."

She sprinted to Bug, wondering if Sonja Backstrom was on the phone with Luke . . . or someone else.

She drove west to the office, realizing she hadn't had to shake up Sonja's poise. The woman was already unraveling. She'd love to find out what Sonja was so desperate to keep hidden.

Traffic on the freeway was backed up, three lanes of cars idled and spewing out exhaust. By the time she pulled into the firm's parking garage, the sun had set.

She dropped her bag on her desk and took off her coat. She was tired and ready to go home, but she needed to make notes while her meeting with Sonja was fresh on her mind.

She saved the file and checked her email. Jenny had sent the name of a pro bono attorney for Alima Matthews.

When Alima answered Claire's call, Emir was crying in the background. Claire gave her the lawyer's contact information, and then, Alima surprised Claire by telling her Amanda Tutwiler had paid for her husband's funeral.

With what? Claire thought sarcastically.

She wished Alima the best and returned to culling through her emails.

Rafe sent a message with a sad-faced emoji. The gray Accord was rented with a fake ID.

Another lead that didn't pan out.

She locked up the office and drove home worrying about the Accord and the wisdom of getting involved with Alfonsi.

What if Alfonsi had asked questions and tripped a wire bringing the man in the gray Accord to her street?

When she turned on Zuni, the Accord wasn't there, and neither was Kirwin's car. The house was dark.

She drove up the driveway as close to the house as she could and hurried to the front door. Once inside with the door bolted shut behind her, she snapped on lights as she walked through the house.

The kitchen looked like she'd left it this morning and the towels in the bathroom were dry. Maybe Kirwin had friends—it still surprised her how little she knew about him—and they were having a guy's night out.

She texted him, but he didn't answer.

She heated leftover Chinese food and watched television, one ear cocked, listening for Kirwin's car.

Around ten, she turned off the TV and phoned him. He didn't pick up and she left a voice mail.

Sleep didn't come.

CHAPTER FOURTEEN

When her alarm went off, Claire pulled on a tatty old robe and walked into the living room.

Kirwin hadn't come home.

She raised one slat in the front blinds and checked the street. The gray Accord was nowhere in sight, and she didn't know if that was a good sign or not. She called Kirwin and it went straight to voicemail.

She checked the bookshelf in the living room. Yep, Eleanor's urn was still there. Kirwin hadn't taken off for good. He'd never leave her behind.

She got ready for work and drove to the office on autopilot, worrying about Kirwin. She wished she'd wheedled out of him what scared him enough to leave Chicago. She also wished she could stop worrying about him. It wasn't like he returned the favor.

In her office, she called Kirwin's cell again. Still, no answer. He'd been missing for less than a day.

Here she was on Day 4 of a big case, and Kirwin does his disappearing act. She was mad at herself because she felt guilty for feeling angry at him.

She flipped through the Tutwiler case file and reread the notes she'd made after talking with Hawkins.

Hawkins had acted like a bird dog pointing to the Backstroms. Was he just protecting Amanda and deflecting attention from her?

Claire thought Allerton was all lime and salt, no tequila, and Amanda was an immature girl. Neither of them could have pulled this off separately or together.

But she couldn't pin the murder on anyone else. Yet.

She wrote *Backstroms* and underlined it. Did Hawkins know more than he told her?

Luke had no money to pay for a killer, and with his debt load, no bank in their right mind would loan him a dime. Truck discovered Luke's company was scraping by every month barely paying its bills. While Luke and Sonja both received a salary, their individual checking accounts were scraping the bottom by month's end. Claire wondered if Sonja knew Luke had heavy gambling losses at the Machias.

A smart guy could hide income, and Millennium's books might be cooked. Luke could be siphoning off cash but proving it would take a court-ordered financial audit and there wasn't enough evidence to get one from a judge. Yet.

Her frustration was building. She doodled circles around Sonja and Luke Backstrom's names, coming up with nothing new.

She tossed the pencil on her desk. There was nothing left to do but take a soaring leap, maybe right into thin air, but she was giving herself points for creativity.

She picked up her phone. "Can you meet me in your office in half an hour?" she asked Truck.

"Babe come on down. I'm holding office hours right now."

Claire pulled into the stream of traffic and headed for Colfax Avenue. She found a parking spot a half a block from Kwan's Bar.

Sure enough, Truck was sitting in his booth drinking a beer. When he saw her, he broke out in a big grin.

"What liquid refreshment would the lady like?" he asked as she sat.

"Too early for me," Claire said.

"Not even a Bloody Mary? Ah, c'mon."

Claire shook her head. "I want a DNA sample from Luke Backstrom. Can you get me in the Machias as waitstaff? I'll lift a glass he used."

"Babe you don't have to go all Nancy Drew on me. I got people. But stealing a glass he used is not the way you want to go with this." He leaned back. "Trying to get DNA off a glass or a can gives you a fifty percent success rate. What you want is the gross stuff, ear wax, mucous or dried blood on a tissue, nail clippings, razor, toothbrush. That's where you get your sample. Then, you got a ninety-five percent chance of lifting a nice little string of DNA."

Truck's storehouse of knowledge always surprised her. "I'd have to break into his house to get that."

Truck smiled. "You really need to relax. I got this. What lab do you want me to send the sample to?"

"Biologics Lab in Aurora. I already told them the sample's coming and it's a rush job. Use my name when it's delivered."

He laughed and slapped his palm down on the table. "You were sure I could pull it off."

"Yep, and there's one more thing. Hack into Biologics and get the report on the DNA sample taken from Tutwiler's killer. Strip out all indication the sample was analyzed by Biologics and put another lab's name on it and email it to me. I told Biologics I would be sending them a DNA report to compare the new sample to."

Truck frowned. "If Luke's DNA matches the crime scene sample, no court's going to give a shit. Fruit of the poisonous tree."

"I know that," Claire said.

"Babe, I love it when you start pullin' shit out of thin air." He tossed back the last of his beer. "Office hours is over. I got work to do."

Truck sauntered over to the bar and kissed Mi Sun before he slipped out the back door.

Claire went back to work.

She didn't know who Truck's other customers were, but Mi Sun must. Maybe the Kwan family were the people Truck referred to when he said he had 'people.' Maybe, he and the Kwans were one big happy family, running a bar, hacking, and breaking and entering, and all living upstairs. Cozy.

All she knew was Truck's people better keep their mouths shut.

Claire had been in her office only minutes when Marsh buzzed.

"You have a minute to meet?"

"Sure."

Marsh couldn't know about the breaking and entering and the hacking job, could he?

He was waiting for her when she came in. "Day four. What do you have?"

Good he doesn't know a thing.

She told him about her visit with Mrs. Backstrom.

"Sounds like a woman courting a breakdown," he said. "I heard over at the courthouse Brewster's custody hearing is this morning. A case like that will divert a man's attention. Is he on top of the investigation?"

"The case is moving forward." Claire would have covered for Rafe even though it wasn't "The cops found the Big Pies' car yesterday, and took a DNA sample."

Marsh didn't seem impressed. He leaned forward, his hands clasped together on the top of his desk. "I have the responsibility to settle Tutwiler's estate within a reasonable period. Have you found anything that makes you think Amanda isn't squeaky clean? She's pressing me to at least file the will with the court."

"There's no evidence she killed him."

"What about Allerton?"

"If you never met Allerton and you heard the story of him leaving his wife and kid and coming to Denver, you'd think, *Wow, he's good for it*," Claire said. "It's not that I don't like Allerton for it. If he were indicted, we'd kill two birds with one stone, solve our case and protect Amanda, but he's a player, not a risk taker. He didn't have to take the risk of killing Tutwiler, he knew Amanda would inherit at some point. Allerton's wife controls the money, and she had no beef with Tutwiler. Allerton had no money to hire a hit man, and neither did Amanda."

"Good analysis. Remind me to use you as a second at my next court case. Who hired the hit?"

"I don't know. Hawkins says Tutwiler had a very quiet year, no threats, and no hate mail. He thinks the murder is linked to the bridge scandal."

"I don't care why Tutwiler was killed," Marsh shot back. "I need you to clear Amanda's name. What did you find out about Luke Backstrom?"

"He's up to his ears in debt."

Marsh sighed.

She knew what was coming. He always sighed before he asked for a favor.

"Have you done any fence-mending with her?" he asked. "She holds you responsible for nosing into her business."

Claire was not going to apologize for snooping. It was her job. "I'll give her a call and take her to lunch."

Jenny knocked on his door and stuck her head in. "You're nine o'clock is here."

Claire returned to her office with plenty on her plate. Make nice with Amanda, find Kirwin, find the killer. Piece of cake.

She called Kirwin's boss. He hadn't seen Kirwin and he hadn't called in sick.

Kirwin was sleeping on her living room floor, and she didn't even really know *him.*

She was calling the last of the hospitals to see if he had been admitted when Rafe called her.

He was almost gloating with his good news. "We got the gun, a Smith and Wesson semiautomatic. Vice took it off a gang member in a meth bust. The bullets from the test fire are a match to the bullets the ME took out of Tutwiler and Matthews."

"That's great news. What about fingerprints?"

"That's the crap news. The only prints forensics could lift are the tweeker's. He claims he found it in a dumpster behind a convenience store."

"Which one?"

"Guy's a meth head. He can't find his own dick. I got nothing to take to the DA. I'm so damned desperate, I swabbed the meth head's mouth to see if his DNA is a match to the DNA we took from the car."

"Don't get your hopes up," Claire said.

They said their goodbyes.

She didn't tell Rafe about Kirwin's disappearing act. Rafe had his own problems at work and home.

She called the Denver morgue. They didn't have a John Doe that matched Kirwin's description, but she didn't feel any better. His body could be at the bottom of a mountain pass or dumped in the middle of a beet field.

She scrolled the contacts list on her phone.

Dan Alfonsi answered on the first ring.

"This is Claire Callahan. Kirwin's disappeared. Have you found out anything about what he was doing in Chicago?"

"Yeah, this morning. You need to report him missing as soon as we get off the phone. The cops arrested a couple of Outlaw Hustlers for extortion and narcotics distribution. Billy the Nose runs the Hustlers, and Kirwin has done favors for the Nose over the years. Could be trouble for Kirwin."

"What kind of favors?"

"You better hope he was only running messages," Alfonsi said. "The Hustlers sell cocaine out of a gelato shop on the south side of town. The word on the street is someone in the Hustlers is feeding the cops information, and the Nose has it in his head it's Kirwin."

"Oh, God. Why?"

"Because the day they were arrested, the Nose and his crew were meeting in the backroom of the gelato shop. In walks Kirwin carrying a package. Minutes after Kirwin slipped out the back, the cops came through the front, and busted the Nose and his crew."

"Do you think the Hustlers have Kirwin?"

"They didn't have to come to Denver for him," Alfonsi said. "The Nose has a cousin in Denver who is an East Niners Owls. He goes by Porky Blue Eyes. His real name is Frank Castelle. You need to let the cops handle this. Kirwin's in way over his head. A couple of Niners were sent down for murder last year. Turn it over to the cops and stay out of it. I'll be in touch."

Alfonsi hung up.

Claire looked at the notes she'd scribbled while Alfonsi talked. She knew where The Niners operated, on the east side of downtown in Montbello.

If Billy the Nose thought Kirwin was the snitch, Kirwin might already be dead.

She called Marsh's extension. She wanted a few hours of personal time.

He listened and said, "We don't pick our families Claire, and what they do with their lives is no reflection on who we are. Go do what you have to do. Let me know if the firm can help."

With his blessing, she left.

On the way to the Sixth Street station, she called Sargent Daniels in Missing Persons. She'd worked with him before, and she felt comfortable with him. Daniels was on old hand and he had good instincts.

Her emotions were pinging between anger and embarrassment. Kirwin was a lousy son and a non-existent father, and now, he'd barged into her life needing help just when she was working the biggest case of her career.

She shut down her pity party when she remembered what Grandma Callie always said: *Family looks after family.*

She parked in front of the Sixth Division and went inside.

She asked the officer working the reception desk for Sargent Daniels, and he buzzed her through.

Daniels expressed his sympathy when Claire told him Kirwin was missing.

He asked for a picture, but the only picture Claire

had ever seen was a black and white photo of him when he was about six years old, so she described him to Daniels.

"Nearly six feet tall, fifty pounds overweight, close-trimmed white hair, clean shaven, in his mid-sixties. Oh, and when he smiles, he has a dimple on his left cheek."

"Identifying marks?" Daniels asked.

"Other than the dimple? None that I know of. He was wearing jeans, a red-checked flannel shirt and white trainers the last time I saw him. He works at a warehouse on Speer. I have the number, but I don't know the name of the place."

Daniels jotted down the warehouse number and Kirwin's cell number. "Has he ever been arrested?"

"Probably."

She described Kirwin's car, a Mercury sedan the size of a boat, four doors, a rusting white paint job with Illinois plates.

"Any reason to suspect foul play?"

She squared her shoulders and fudged her answer. "He never complained to me, but I'm worried. He's always home by the time I get there."

Daniels assured her he'd do his best. "Don't worry, we'll find him."

She thanked him and left. Why do people always say 'Don't worry' when something awful has happened?

She couldn't sit on her butt while the cops looked for Kirwin, nor could she search all the Niners territory. They controlled a lot of land south of the Interstate.

She'd had to tell Marsh Kirwin was a runner for the Nose, and of course, Alfonsi knew, but she was not calling Rafe for help. She would not have her personal life humming on the cop grapevine.

She was fuming at Kirwin for putting her this position. She needed help.

She called Mac McNally.

"It's Claire. I need some information."

"Now what?" he asked.

She poured out the story of the Niners.

McNally was all business. "Yeah, I know the Niners. I worked with the Aurora police to get an indictment against one of them. Their crew chief is Porky Blue Eyes and he and his crew hang at the Taco Hut on the corner of Tejon and Seventy. The cops think they operate their business out of there. A redhead like you is going to stick out like fresh meat. Do you want me to ride along?"

"Thanks, Mac, I got this covered. What does Porky look like?"

"Three hundred pounds of tattooed fat. He's got an owl tat that runs up his neck onto the side of his face and across his shaved head. Call me if you need me," Mac said and hung up.

Claire tapped in the code to the gun safe in the bottom drawer of her desk. The Glock's small size tucked snugly in the pancake holster at the back of her pants.

She pulled a light windbreaker on over the gun and left the office.

Cruising Peoria, the main street bisecting the crime-ridden Montbello neighborhood, she thought the neighborhood looked tough enough even the crows might wear ankle bracelets and carry knives in their beaks. She turned right at the next intersection on Tejon and drove past the Taco Hut, taking a good look. No one was murdering anyone in front of the restaurant, so she circled the block and parked across the street from the Hut.

She locked Bug and jaywalked to the Hut.

The Hut didn't look much bigger than her duplex.

Made of adobe and painted the color of pan-fried ground meat, a web of fine cracks looked like spider webs running through the mud.

The carved front door was standing open, only a flimsy screen door separated the business from the sidewalk. The smell of frying onions and the heavy bass of gangsta rap spilled out on the street.

The screen door banged shut behind her. She stood in the entry, her eyes adjusting to the gloom.

Six men sat around the center table. They were colored up, black on red, and their bared arms had prison tats of crudely drawn owls.

She was silhouetted in the entry, and all their eyes locked on her.

One guy made a circle with his forefinger and thumb and thrust his other forefinger in and out of the circle. There was an orgy of laughter and fist bumping.

They were still laughing when she walked over to the fat one with a tattoo of an owl on his neck and an owl's wing tatted over his shaved head. It didn't look too bad, almost artsy.

She stood in front of him, and the men shut up and leered at her.

"I'm looking for Frank Castelle."

The fat one shook his head and scowled. "Never heard of him."

Claire put a scrap of paper with her cell phone on the table. "If you see him, have him give me a call. It's about a friend of mine, Kirwin."

He didn't reach for her card.

She tapped the tabletop. "The Nose sends his regards from the Cook County Jail."

One guy jerked his head toward Frank while a couple of others shot him stares.

Claire backed away from the table. "Tell Frank he needs to talk to me."

Her heart was banging in her chest, but she forced herself to stroll out the door.

Claire was rolling toward the freeway before she could take a deep breath. With the Nose in jail, maybe Frank would call to find out what else she knew.

She returned to her office to tackle another problem, mending fences with Amanda.

For all her exasperation with Amanda, she was fond of her. The girl was only a year out from a terrifying experience, and she had fallen under the spell of the slick-talking Allerton. She deserved better.

Claire picked up her cell, then put it down.

Why would she listen to me?

She didn't have a good answer, but she did have a job to do.

She called Amanda and it went to voice mail.

Before she could put her phone down, it buzzed an alert.

A text from Amanda: *don't call me.*

Claire called her again and was surprised when Amanda answered.

"Hello, Claire." Amanda was cool and wary. "You just can't quit making trouble, can you? James lost his job because of you, and Elizabeth threatened to throw his stuff in the street if he didn't get there and pick it up."

"How are you?"

"Oh, what a stupid thing to ask. Just get out of my life. You and Marsh both. I'm not a kid anymore. Clear my name and get the estate settled and then we're finished."

At least Amanda hadn't fired the firm on the spot.

CHAPTER FIFTEEN

It was after five and Claire was dragging her feet at the thought of going home to an empty house. Just thinking about seeing Kirwin's messy bed on the floor and Eleanor's ashes on the shelf made her shiver.

Was he dead like Eleanor?

Jenny buzzed her. "St. Joseph's emergency room is on line two for you."

That made her lungs stop. She was already on her feet, holding her keys in one hand and her bag on her shoulder when she answered the phone. "This is Claire Callahan."

Claire didn't catch the woman's name, just her words tumbling out and flaying her soul with tiny claws.

Kirwin had been brought in by ambulance, and her business card was tucked in his wallet.

"How is he?" Claire asked.

"I can't release any information except to family."

"I'm on my way."

She ran past Jenny. "It's Kirwin. I'll call you when I know something."

As she drove, she kept telling herself that St. Jo's was

a trauma center with a good reputation. Kirwin would be fine.

She followed the signs to the Emergency Room parking lot. She was out of Bug and running toward the entrance.

The automatic doors swung open, and too her right was a packed waiting room. To her left, a counter with two women, one on the phone, the other watching Claire.

"Can I help you?" the clerk asked.

"I'm here for Kirwin Callahan. I'm his daughter." Claire flipped out her license. "He's my father." The words sounded strange in her ears. Technically, it was true. Emotionally was a whole other matter.

The clerk glanced at Claire's identification and beckoned her. "Come this way."

She led Claire through swinging doors into the emergency room and said, "Wait here, I'll find a nurse."

The curtains blocked prying eyes but not the whispered conversations, the cries, and an occasional drunken shout. Then she heard someone in the patient bed nearest her vomiting, and the hot, acrid smell rolled into the hallway.

The clerk returned with a nurse who introduced herself. "I'm Jo Goldstein. Mr. Callahan is in our major trauma room."

"Is he going to be okay?"

"It looks to me like he took a beating from an expert. Come this way."

Claire's heart sank. The hospital had to call the police when a victim was brought in. Would Kirwin be so doped up, he'd incriminate himself?

She was calling the firm as she followed the nurse. She told Jenny Kirwin needed a lawyer.

"I'm on it. I'll talk to Mr. Marsh and call you back. Hang in there, we're all pulling for you and your dad."

"Thanks."

The nurse stopped before a cubicle and pulled the curtains back.

Claire walked to the bedside and wasn't sure it was Kirwin.

His face was swollen, the right side of his jaw had a lump the size of a baseball, both eyes were black, and his nose flattened. A blood-soaked bandage covered his head above his left ear.

A weary-looking doctor was reading an EKG strip. He didn't acknowledge they were in the room until the nurse said, "This is his daughter, Claire Callahan."

The doctor introduced himself and said, "He's sustained serious injuries and at his age, they could be life-threatening."

"Do you think he'll die?"

"I'm cautiously optimistic," he said. "He has a ruptured spleen. His left hand is crushed, he has a couple of broken ribs, and he's concussed. Dr. Nguyen is taking him up to surgery. He'll remove the spleen and take care of the bleeding. He's going to have to have surgery on the hand after they get him stabilized. Does he see a doctor for his heart?"

"I don't know. Is there a problem?"

"His EKG shows some atrial fibrillation," he said. "AFib is not uncommon in older people. I'll call an attending on the cardiac service to take a look at him." He smiled. "Don't worry, he's in good hands." The doctor excused himself and left.

There it was again, 'don't worry.' How could she not worry? He looked so vulnerable and now he had heart trouble.

The nurse touched her arm. "You can stay with him until they come to take him to surgery."

Claire hooked a chair with her foot and dragged it over to the bed. She'd heard patients could hear even if they were unconscious.

"Kirwin, I'm here. You're going to be fine. I'm staying right here. Can you hear me?"

He didn't respond.

She stroked his stubbled cheek. He'd been living rough. He smelled sour and his hair was matted in greasy tufts.

She reached over the bed rail and picked up Kirwin's good hand and held it in hers. His pale face was slack, gravity drawing his mouth down and the loose skin on his neck into folds. He looked so old and fragile, and so still.

She couldn't remember ever holding his hand. She ran her finger over the row of callouses at the base of his fingers. Had he held her, comforted her when she was a baby? Had he come home and looked down on her in her crib, happy to see her at the end of the day? Picked her up and held her to his chest?

She didn't know. Her memories were of her parents hauling suitcases out the front door to an old car and then months or years later, showing up out of the blue and hauling their suitcases back through the door. Only to leave again.

Had he kissed her goodbye when he left? Did he tell her to be a good girl for her grandmother?

All she could remember was crying at the front window while he and Eleanor drove away, and Callie trying to distract her with the promise of baking cookies.

What if he dies?

She squeezed his hand. "Don't you die. You can't leave me now. I've been mad at you all my life. I wanted you to tuck me in at night, be there for breakfast, bring a Christmas tree home, do all the things other kids' daddies did. Callie forgave you before she died. I haven't, you can't leave like this."

She dropped his hand. How selfish and entitled. It wasn't about her. He was fighting for his life.

If I cried when they left, I must have felt something for them.

She whispered in his ear, "I'm sorry for what I said. I want you to live. I want us to make memories we can look back on and laugh about later."

A nurse came in on soft-soled shoes and stood at the computer. "We need a little information on Mr. Callahan. What medication is he on?"

Claire shook her head. "I don't know anything about his medical history. We've only seen each other twice in the last twenty-plus years."

The nurse looked up over the keyboard, a flash of sorrow in her eyes. "I'm sorry. We'll take good care of him."

Two orderlies came to take Kirwin to surgery.

The nurse told her the waiting area was on the second floor.

The orderlies rolled Kirwin out, and Claire left the Emergency Room and took the elevator up.

No one was in the waiting area. It was cluttered with overstuffed furniture and tables piled with magazines. Two chairs faced a bank of windows looking out over the rainswept streets. She headed to the windows.

The light rain spattered against the glass. The streetlamps threw hazy pools of yellow light on the streets.

It was quiet, the shock was waning and away from the din of the Emergency room, she could think.

If the Nose had ordered the Niners to beat Kirwin, they'd come after him again if they heard he was alive.

She called Harry Copeland, the ex-cop who owned Eagle Security. She told him Kirwin's story and he agreed to put a man on his door when he was out of surgery and in a private room.

She hoped to God Kirwin hadn't delivered drugs or carried money for the Nose. He'd never make it out of prison alive.

Detective Red Stilinski walked in and said, "Claire, I'm so sorry about your dad." He pulled the other chair closer to her and sat, leaning forward with his long arms hanging between his legs. "Are you up to a few questions?"

"Sure, but I hadn't seen him in over a year. He turned up at my place asking if he could stay a few days ago."

"So, you two aren't close?"

Ya think?

"No, my grandmother raised me."

"She still around?" Red asked.

Claire shook her head.

"Where did you dad move from?"

"Chicago."

"Did he have any enemies up there?"

"I don't know anything about Kirwin's life, period," Claire said. "Where was he found?"

"A shop owner found him in the alley on Havana near East Forty-Seventh."

Kirwin hadn't been far from the Taco Hut where she confronted Porky and the Niners.

"You know what he was doing over there?" Red asked.

Claire shook her head.

"What's a good number where we can reach you?"

Claire wrote her cell on the back of her business card and handed it to him.

He pocketed the card. "I left a message with the nurses to call me when Mr. Callahan wakes up. I have some questions for him."

That sounded ominous. She hoped Marsh found Kirwin a lawyer before he woke up and started yakking.

She didn't have a clue what she was up against and she was weary.

She stumbled over to a sofa and stretched out. Every time she moved the slightest bit, the cushions parted, opening an earthquake-sized crack her hip sank into.

She must have slept because she was startled when she heard: "Ms. Callahan?"

She sat up squinting at the light. "Yes?"

"I'm Dr. Nguyen, I operated on your Dad. He's stable, but I'm concerned about the blow he took to his head. His scans show a skull fracture, a hair-thin line through the skull."

Claire dropped her head in her hands.

"There's good news, too," the doctor said. "There's no splintering of the bone or depression of his skull. It's a simple linear fracture, it should heal by itself, but it will take months. Right now, he's still in surgery, the orthopedic surgeon is working on his hand. The nurse will stay in touch with you." He left.

She wiggled around until she found a comfortable place on the sofa.

She was awakened by, "Babe."

Truck's hand was on her arm. He was squatting on his heels looking at her.

"How are you doing?"

"What time is it?" she answered half asleep.

"Six in the morning. I brought you some coffee and a Danish. All they had left was cheese."

"How did you know?"

"I hear things."

He put his arm around her and hugged her.

They sat that way for a bit until Claire felt she could speak without bawling. Funny how when a friend showed up to be with her, she fell apart and cried.

She took a deep breath and pulled herself together. "He must be up in a room by now."

"I asked downstairs, and they told me they didn't have a Kirwin Callahan registered."

Claire blew out a breath. "That's good, but I don't know how long the ruse will work. Mac sent over security."

"How bad is he?"

Claire explained his injuries.

"They got good docs here." Truck squeezed her shoulder. "You know that business you asked me to take care of? It's done."

"Ohhh." She sighed with relief. "And delivered to the lab?"

Truck grinned. "You gotta ask? Yeah, it's there."

Her phone vibrated in her pocket. Jenny had texted the name and number of an attorney. Abe Guthrie was expecting her call.

"I have to call this guy. He's Kirwin's lawyer."

"I'll be checking with you," Truck said, getting up and leaving.

Claire explained to Guthrie the whole sordid story—the Hustlers, the Niners, the accusation Kirwin was a snitch. Guthrie agreed to provide representation and said he would notify the police he was Kirwin's lawyer.

Rafe walked into the waiting room as she hung up.

"Have they caught the guy who attacked Kirwin?" she asked.

Rafe shook his head. "Why would anyone attack Kirwin?"

"Kirwin had some trouble in Chicago," Claire said

picking her words carefully. "That's why he moved to Denver."

"What kind of trouble?"

"He wouldn't tell me."

"Um, how is he?"

Claire explained his injuries. "Mac's put security on his room."

"Wise choice. Was Kirwin in a gang in Chicago?"

"I don't know."

"Have you hired him a lawyer?"

She nodded. "Abe Guthrie."

"Look Claire, cut your losses. Let a public defender represent Kirwin."

"I don't know that any charges are going to be filed against him. He's the victim."

"You're worried, or you wouldn't have hired a top gun like Guthrie," Rafe said. "Get some rest. I'll call you if I hear anything."

CHAPTER SIXTEEN

THE FALL DRIZZLE WAS JUST HEAVY ENOUGH TO MAKE A mess of the windshield, and the slick streets were clogged with late afternoon traffic. Luke was running the Porsche at less than twenty miles per hour, longing to let her rip and eat up the miles.

Sonja called, frantic and at times incoherent, wheedling a promise out of him to come home.

He wished he still had his condo to escape to. It was hell living at home again, but that wasn't what was keeping him up at nights.

The lenders were watching like vultures to see if he could turn the company around and make them money. The greedy bastards would cut his legs off at his knees if the Market project or the condominiums didn't come in on time and on budget. If he could bring these two projects to the finish line, his name would be solid in the construction world. New deals would be signed, rivers of money would flow in—and best of all, he could get away from his mother and buy his own place.

She was his Achilles' heel. She was on a steady downhill course, fearful, anxious and needy. Her doctor prescribed a cocktail of drugs for anxiety and insomnia. He'd also mentioned to Luke she might benefit from going into a private hospital out of town.

Luke vacillated between thinking he should keep his mom by him where he could keep an eye on her or getting her as far away from Denver as possible. Sonja could start blabbing in a private hospital just as easily in her home. He figured he'd be a loser no matter where she was if she started yapping.

At least, she had quit asking him if he killed Tutwiler. Now she was moaning about how guilty she felt and talking about all the things she'd done for Luke —though when he asked her what *things* she was talking about, she suddenly had nothing to say.

He worried she killed Tutwiler and was losing her mind over it. Though God only knew how a woman like his mother could find someone to kill a man.

He had enough problems demanding his attention, including Mick Donovan.

From a man who never used to pay Luke any attention, Donovan was now breathing down his neck every time he went to the Machias to unwind. Wherever Luke was in the club, Mick turned up with a drink in his hand and would make some comment about how deep the snow was at the top of Ute Pass or some damn thing about the park.

Like a guy in his seventies was interested in outdoor winter sports.

To the rest of the players, it sounded like inane chatter, but Luke knew better. Luke was sure Donovan knew he'd put out a hit on Tutwiler. Luke was as sure of it as he was that Donovan was the go-between separating him from the hitman.

More than anything, Luke wanted to beat the shit

out of the old man for not giving him a refund, but he was too afraid to ask.

Donovan was making veiled threats about what would happen if Luke didn't pay his gambling debt. Yet, Donovan had his 50K in his pocket.

If he had the balls, he'd tell Donovan to deduct the 50K from what he owed him, but he wasn't going to cross Mick. He believed the rumors that Donovan was still connected with the Smaldone family. If Luke couldn't get his hands on some money, he'd never be free of Mick Donovan or the Smaldone family.

Luke pulled into the circle drive of his childhood home. He loved this property and always thought he would raise his family here. But no chance of that now. They needed to sell the house to raise cash for his mounting debts.

The lacy green vines crawling up the courtyard walls still had a few fragrant white flowers. The frost hadn't dipped into the sheltered area and nipped them. He used to play here in the shelter of the porch, and their fragrance brought back happy memories.

He let himself in with his key and called to his mother.

Sonja answered from her sitting room. He walked through the entryway past a portrait of the three of them, his mom and dad, and him just after he had graduated from high school.

Better times than now.

Luke found his mom in the little sitting room off her bedroom.

Still in her bathrobe and slippers, a bowl of congealed soup and a drying sandwich sat on the table next to her. She looked like a bag lady, hair uncombed, eyes rheumy and unfocused.

She braced her elbow on the table, and put her hand

across her forehead, covering her eyes. "I can't do this anymore. It's too much."

The faraway clinic was looking like a better option.

Luke pulled a chair around in front of her and sat down. He unbuttoned his coat and leaned forward.

"Tell me about it." He expected her to say she had hired the gunman who killed Tutwiler. "Get it all out on the table Mom, and we can deal with it."

Instead, she said: "That PI came around to see me. The one you said talked to you. Claire somebody."

"What did you tell her?"

"Nothing, I swear. But she knows something. I could tell."

"What do you think she knows?"

Sonja held her head in her hands, weeping.

Luke knew how to handle his mother's episodes. He cooed and clucked over her like a mother hen. Patted her shoulder, kissed her cheek, and told her things would work out. "They always do. Let me help you with what's bothering you."

She raised her head as if she would tell him. Her lips parted, and then, she clamped her mouth closed.

So close to finding out what was on her mind, and then boom, back to la-la land. She was too emotionally fragile, and Luke didn't know who else she was blabbing and blubbering to, but he intended to find out.

"I think you need to get away and rest," he said. "Remember we talked about the spa in Santa Fe? You always like that place. Or you could go to the private clinic your doctor mentioned."

She shook her head. "I won't leave you here by yourself. Not when the job site is closed down, and the police are investigating. What if the police never find out who killed Tutwiler? You'll always be under suspicion."

He avoided telling her she would also remain under suspicion.

"Can't help that. You and I know we didn't kill him. Right?"

She wouldn't look at him. When she tried to pick up her tea, her hands shook so badly the cup rattled against the saucer. She put it down and folded her hands in her lap.

Now was as good a time as any to find out who she'd been talking to.

"Have you talked to anyone about what's worrying you?" Luke asked.

She shook her head.

"Mom, you know we're on a family cell phone plan. I can see the phone numbers. Who are you talking to up in Weld County?"

"An old friend, we went to school together." Sonja wouldn't look at him when she said it. "She and her husband recently moved back there, and she's lonely."

"You two are burning up the minutes. She calls you nearly every day, but you don't talk long. What's going on?"

"I don't think that's any of your business," Sonja said softly.

"Did you tell her about Tutwiler's murder?"

"She saw it in the papers and called me. I didn't say anything more than what was in the news."

He could tell she was lying.

"Have I met this old friend? Did she come down for Dad's funeral?"

"No," Sonja said, lying again. "She and her husband were having troubles. She thought he was going to leave her."

Luke leaned in close, his head level with hers. "Mom, you can't talk to anyone about Tutwiler's death.

Not your girlfriend, not your grief counselor, not your doctor."

She nodded her head like an obedient child.

Luke had never seen his mother like this. Not even after Dad died. She looked like a ragdoll pulled apart by two terriers named Guilt and Grief.

But Luke knew an opportunity when it presented itself. "I need your help."

Her hand snaked around his arm and held him with a vice grip. "Do you know what I've already done for you? How can you ask for more?"

"What are you talking about? Whatever is bothering you, you've blown it way out of proportion. Unless you're not telling me something."

"No, you have no idea. The years lost, the time we could have had together. All gone."

He gripped her arm. "Mom," he said seething with impatience and trying to keep it hidden. "You and Dad had years together. He killed himself. It's not your fault."

She took a deep calming breath and pulled herself together. "Yes, of course. Nothing to do with me." She tried to smile. "That's what the grief counselor said, the family is never to blame when a loved one takes his life."

He let go of her arm and noticed the faint bruising.

"I need help. The company needs cash."

She shook her head. "I've given you all the money I have." Then she started crying again. "I don't have anything left, but you."

"Where did you get the money you gave me a couple of weeks ago?"

"I cashed out an investment account your father and I had. There's no more. Dave poured all the money back into the business. I begged him to set some aside for our retirement." She shrugged. "But he wouldn't do it."

Luke had caught her in another lie. "Earlier, you said the money you gave me was your inheritance from your folks. Which is it? Your inheritance or an investment account you and Dad had?"

She looked surprised. "What does it matter? It's all gone."

"Then we have to sell the house. It's paid for, and the market is hot for older homes near downtown."

One look at her face and he knew he had to offer her something to get her to agree to sign the papers.

"I'll buy you a new house," he said, "whatever you want once I get on my feet. I'm in a bind right now, but things will change. OSHA still has the job site shut down, but when OSHA finally gets off its ass and clears us, it'll take me some time to hire men and get rolling. But Mom, the bank wants their money. We could lose it all, the Market project and the condominiums. We're at a tipping point. The money from the house will save the business for both of us."

And get Mick Donovan off my ass, he thought. Donovan set the vig at 18% on his gambling debt. Luke paid down the debt every week, but by the next Friday, the vig had him in a bigger hole.

Cashing in on the house would buy him time. That's all he needed. He was a smart guy. He could figure out the rest.

He took both her hands in his. "Look at me. I promised Dad I'd take care of you and I will."

Her mouth was quivering. "You were raised in this house. It's our home. Isn't there something else you can do?"

Luke shook his head. "No bank is going to loan me more money."

Sonja's shoulders sagged. "But . . . where will I live?"

Oh, sweet victory.

If his mother was thinking about where she was going to live, she'd capitulated on selling the house.

"We'll find a nice house, big enough for the two of us and then when the business is pulling in money, I'll buy you whatever you want. I promise. You trust me to take care of you, don't you?"

She nodded. "I felt bad when you had to sell your condo and move in here."

"I wouldn't have had it any other way," he lied. "And the money staved off the banks for a while. But now, we're in a real tight spot. We need to list the house as soon as possible. This week."

Sonja sat up straight. "So fast?"

"I think so." He nodded and smiled. "I'll do everything I can to make it as painless as possible. Why don't you start looking for a new place today?" He stood, then leaned over and kissed her cheek.

He left her crying, and he hated that, but a huge weight lifted off his shoulders.

Sonja watched Luke walk away. She'd have to leave the beautiful little sitting room she'd decorated herself. She'd built a wonderful life in this house, and now she had to give it up.

Double-damn Dave for screwing up her life.

Who would she be without this house as her home? The tentpole of her identity in society was this house. Brick by brick she built a comfortable life with Dave's money. The right house in the right neighborhood, the best schools for Luke, the membership in the Denver Country Club.

She'd reinvented herself once, and she resented having to do it again, and this time, she wasn't climbing up the ladder of wealth. She feared she was on a long slide down to the mean obscurity Dave had plucked her from.

Maybe there wouldn't be any more good times.

Her family had been rough and poor, and the worst of it was the grinding hopelessness.

Her mom had been lucky. She died young, but she'd left Sonja with her Dad, a miserable old sod with a nasty temper.

She grew up shivering under the covers in her room, listening to her Dad yelling and the sound of crashing plates and sharp opened-handed slaps.

She'd dreamed of her knight in shining armor whisking her away.

And then one night, Dave Backstrom walked into the honky-tonk where she was a waitress. A construction engineer with a road crew building a new highway over the pass.

Sonja knew that when the road was finished, he'd be gone, and she had every intention of going with him. She did everything but pole dance buck-naked to get his attention.

And then, one night a week before he was leaving, he asked her to marry him. She jumped into his arms.

Of course, her ride out of town with her knight came with conditions. Over the decades, she had kept her promise to cut ties with her kin and keep her mouth shut about them.

In return, he promised her he wouldn't hold her lack of education and rough ways against her. But he did. Every fight, every disagreement, Dave tossed her low-class ways in her face.

In public, Dave's censure was more subtle—an arched brow, a cautioning hand on her arm, but he always let her know she wasn't worthy of being his wife.

When she confronted him about the affair with Lucy, he'd grinned and told her he loved Lucy because she was refined.

She stayed with him because he had money, and he would use it to take Luke from her.

She even held up her end of the bargain when her Dad died. She never mentioned his passing to Dave or Luke.

None of the past mattered now. Dave was dead, and she didn't have to think about pleasing him.

If only the calls would quit coming, she might get some sleep and think more clearly. She didn't answer them anymore. What was the point? What was done was done.

Sonja went into her bedroom and collected all the pill bottles. Her brain was so fogged from the medication, she couldn't think straight.

She flushed them all down the toilet and hid the bottles in the trash.

She sensed it building. She knew it was coming for her. A wildfire smoldering in the underbrush, licking at the dry grass. It would leap to the treetops and roar through the forest, burning the wall she kept around her and laying her bare.

What if Luke hated her when he found out?

She'd never see her boy again, never hold her grandbabies in her arms.

LUKE PROPPED his feet on the desk in the study and sipped his brandy.

He was no shrink, but even he knew his mother was hiding something, and it was eating her alive. How in the hell would she react if she knew about his gambling debt, or the Buckner investment, or the bag of money he dropped on the Ute Trail? The doc would have to cart her off in a straitjacket.

She'd been lying to him. When she handed over the check a couple of weeks ago, she said it was her inheritance from her old man. That certainly surprised him. She'd never talked about her family.

Now, she said it was money from an investment account. He had access to every statement with Dave's name on it and there was no investment account. Why was she lying?

He took a cigar out of the humidor and snipped the end with the little guillotine. He held it in his mouth, tasting the aromatic tobacco before he lighted it. With the first pull on the cigar, he felt the tension ease. He leaned back in his chair, closed his eyes and gave himself over to the joy of smoking. How could something this good still be legal in this country?

He ran the numbers in his head, figuring the sale of the house would clear his debt to Donovan and tide the business over until he had crews working again. Once the Market project was near completion, his banker would loan him cash to build his next project.

He tapped off the long worm of ash.

The Buckner investment fiasco had cost him a cool $100,000. He could beat himself up about getting taken to the cleaners, or he could get out there and make more money.

He'd never been one to look over his shoulder and berate himself, and he wasn't going to start now. He'd double what he lost, just as soon as he was shy of Donovan.

Donovan had threatened him with a beating if he didn't pay up.

Luke asked him, "What is this? Chicago in the twenties?"

Donovan didn't even crack a smile.

The last time he'd seen him, Donovan said: "My friend, you need my silence, and I haven't decided what that's going to cost you."

It had scared the shit out of him.

Luke balanced the cigar on the edge of the ashtray, picked up the phone and called the most successful real estate group in Denver. He arranged to have an agent come to the house.

Fat lot of good his plans would do if he couldn't get Sonja to sign the contract. And showing the house would be a real bitch since she'd taken to lying in bed most of the day, or sitting in the chair, staring into space.

The pressure was eating him alive. If the house didn't sell quickly, he might be in a hospital, and his mother would be begging her friends for a place to live.

What did she know he didn't?

He'd already gone through every scrap of paper he'd found in his Dad's study and looked at everything in his bank box. Luke had turned the house and the office upside down and hadn't discovered any secrets worth lying about.

He was near the end of his tether doing what his Dad's will requested. Sonja was to receive a generous monthly stipend and a percentage of the profits for the duration of her life. He'd shot through the money from the sale of his condo taking care of his mother. She'd have to scale her living expenses down a notch or two, and if the house didn't sell, her sweetheart deal his Dad set up was going down the drain just like he was.

He was fast losing patience with her. He was busting his hump twelve hours a day while she idled in bed. He damn well knew when she gave him that first bundle of money, it came out of her inheritance. There were no investment accounts in Dave's name. She was holding out on him. She never worked a day in her sweet life, and she had no right to treat him this way.

Part of his troubles were of his own making and he could admit that to himself, but he was working his ass off to make it right.

He was in big trouble. Had he missed anything when he searched the house?

He sat back smoking and thinking.

He'd been a snoop as a kid. He'd looked in every cubby hole in the house and through all the drawers and the pockets of their coats. Before middle school age, he'd graduated to pilfering money from his parents and from the stack of bills the maid kept taped to the underside of one of her dresser drawers.

No one seemed to notice, or in the maid's case, she wanted her job enough to keep quiet about the theft. His most significant find was jerked out of his hands before he could lift the lid.

When his mom caught him red-handed clutching the carved camphor wood chest Dad had brought home to her from a business trip to Asia, she tucked it away and he'd never seen it again.

She'd had a hissy fit and made him promise to stop going through other people's things. He dutifully agreed, thinking he'd find the chest the next time she left the house.

He never saw it again.

What did she have in there that had to be hidden?

He climbed the stairs and waited outside her door until he heard the shower running. He walked into Sonja's sitting room and systematically searched it and the bedroom.

At the bottom of her closet, under a stack of photo

albums and empty shoe boxes, he found the chest. As a kid, he'd poked through her closet many times. She must have kept moving the chest from place to place.

He took it to his study and locked the door behind him.

On the lid of the chest, intricately carved sampans floated on a choppy sea, and on the front, tiny hunched-over Chinese men sat under a pagoda, the roof's corners turned up to the sky.

He flipped open the lid, and the lingering odor of medicated chest rub mixed with the smell of old paper.

CHAPTER SEVENTEEN

Claire came home and crashed, catching a few hours of restless sleep. She awoke tired and grumpy, reaching for her buzzing phone before her brain was fully in gear.

A text from the floor nurse reported Kirwin's vital signs were good and he was somewhat conscious.

Thanks, Claire texted back. *What room is he in?*

407

A cup of coffee later, her brain was fully functioning, and she gave Kirwin's new attorney a call, and told Abe Guthrie his new client was awake. She also mentioned she'd hired a PI from Chicago.

Guthrie said, "Alfonsi can't share information without your agreement, so give him a call and tell him I'm Kirwin's attorney and give him my number." Then he surprised her: "Because you work for Charles Marsh, you'll get the friends and family discount. Don't sweat my bill."

What a relief. Criminal defense lawyers in Guthrie's league didn't come cheap.

She thanked him and hung up, then called Alfonsi.

She told him about the attack on Kirwin. "Abe Guthrie is Kirwin's lawyer. Please share whatever you have with him."

Alfonsi said, "Right, I'll give him a call. Shit's hit the fan up here. Early this morning the cops pulled a Ford Escort out of the Chicago River, and Sammy Torrio was in the trunk with his tongue cut out. I have a cop friend who says Torrio was his informant inside the Hustlers."

"Great . . . well, for Kirwin it's good news, but he's not off the hook for whatever he was running for Billy."

"I have someone who owes me one," Alfonsi said, "I'll get it out of him. Talk to you soon."

When Claire arrived at the hospital, she headed straight to Kirwin's room.

A tall man with a gray buzz-cut stood in front of Kirwin's door, his feet shoulder width apart, his hands hanging loosely at his sides, his eyes roving from one end of the corridor to the other, checking faces.

Claire had her license and ID out by the time she reached him. "I'm Claire Callahan, his daughter."

He glanced at her license and then scrutinized her face. "I'm Zach Kelly, Eagle Security." He stepped aside so she could enter the room.

She found Kirwin sitting up in bed spooning red Jell-O into his mouth. She leaned over and kissed his cheek. "How are you feeling?"

"I've felt better, but I'm breathing."

Claire pulled the visitor's chair closer to the bed.

"Am I going to be okay?" he asked.

"The doc says so. You've had surgery, and they taped up your broken ribs. The knock on your head is going to take some time to heal."

He held up his bandaged hand. "But am I ever going to be able to use this?"

"The surgeon says you'll need a lot of physical therapy. How much use you get back, he's not saying."

"I gotta have my hand to keep my job."

"Let's just concentrate on getting better. Do you want me to call your boss and let him know you'll be off for a while?"

"He won't keep me on," he said glumly, "but yeah, call him. "How'd I get here?"

"You were found unconscious in an alley in Montbello. An ambulance brought you here to St. Joseph's. Do you remember anything?"

He looked away from her. "I left work and stopped for a pack of smokes at the convenience store where I always buy. A couple guys jumped out of a cargo van and dragged me into the back of it." He turned his head to look at her. "It happened so fast. One minute I was on the street and the next I thought I was a goner. They kicked the shit out me. I must have passed out. Next thing I remember, a doc is leaning over me."

"Kirwin, what's going on?"

"These people ain't done with me."

"That's not an answer," Claire said, "but you are safe. I hired security. There's a man right outside your door. What are you mixed up in?"

He spoke so softly she had to lean in to hear him. "Pigeon, I never meant to get you involved."

"That's water under the bridge," she snapped. "Tell me what's going on, so I can help you."

"Billy thinks I done something I didn't. If I could just talk to him, I could set this all straight. We were kids together back in the old neighborhood, and in the Army together until they kicked him out. He'd set up shop in Chicago by the time I was discharged, and he sent word for me to come join him."

How much worse could this be? He had been working for Billy the Nose for decades.

"What kind of work was Billy doing?"

He waggled his good hand from side to side. "A little of this, a little of that."

Claire lost her patience. "Billy the Nose is head of the biggest crime family in the Midwest."

Kirwin's face turned red to the roots of his hair.

"He and three of his crew are sitting in jail right now," she added.

"Getting charged don't mean you're guilty," Kirwin said. "You don't understand. Me and Eleanor and Billy go way back to when we were kids. Me and Eleanor did favors for him once in a while. He fixed our car and bought us groceries. He's my friend."

Claire shook her head. "That makes no sense. He put you in the hospital."

He turned his head to the wall. "I can sort it out with Billy if I can talk to him. He don't know the truth."

"You were a runner for Billy, and you delivered something to him at the gelato shop. Now, you're in the hospital."

He looked surprised. "How do you know about that?"

"I'm an investigator. I investigate. What happened?"

"A man called me and said I was to make a delivery to Billy. He told me to leave my car unlocked while I was at work. I did, and when I got off work, my car was locked up and there was a big mailing envelope on the passenger seat. You know one of those brown ones with the clasp on the back?"

She nodded.

"A sticky note on it said to take it to the gelato shop."

"You weren't worried that it was a setup?" Claire asked.

"Nah, I got all my directions over the phone just like that."

"What was in the envelope?"

He shook his head. "Don't work like that. I never peeked, and Billy didn't open it in front of me. My job was to hand it off. I did and then I went out the back door."

"All those years and you never looked inside one of those envelopes? Really?"

He shrugged. "Billy told me not to. He's an important man. Most times I thought it was written messages. Billy's paranoid about phones. Anyway, that day at the shop, I heard sirens coming from everywhere. I ran down the alley, jumped a fence, and made it back to my car and drove straight to Denver. Billy must think I sicced the cops on him."

"Did you ever run money or drugs for Billy?"

"I told you, I never looked." His eyes searched her face. "You gotta help me."

"The cops are going to ask you what was in the envelope you passed to Billy."

He shook his head. "I can't talk about that."

"You have to. Sammy Torrio was hauled out of the Chicago River this morning with his tongue cut out."

His eyes bugged out. "Little Sammy's dead?"

She stood and said, "Yeah, Little Sammy was a snitch for a Chicago cop. The Hustlers are cleaning house. If you want to live, talk to your lawyer. Abe Guthrie will be here this morning. Take his advice." She walked to the door and looked over her shoulder. "I'll check on you later."

She took the elevator down to parking.

She was getting into Bug when she saw Rafe, looking grim and headed her way.

He opened the passenger side door and climbed in

beside her. "Thought I might find you at the hospital." How is he?"

"Kirwin's out of surgery and stable. Guthrie's meeting with him this morning," Claire said warily.

"When were you planning on telling me Kirwin worked for Billy the Nose?"

"I didn't know until yesterday." Claire sensed she was on dangerous ground. "I was trying to protect him." Even to her, the explanation sounded lame.

"You can't protect him from the Hustlers and a lone man from Eagle Security can't either."

"He's too old to go to prison," she blurted.

"If you know something he should go to prison for, you're withholding information from a cop."

Claire groaned. "He was a runner for the Nose, and he won't say or doesn't know what he delivered."

"You can bet your ass someone in the Nose's organization does," Rafe said, "and they'll roll over on Kirwin to save their hide. Red knows Little Sammy's dead. Red's a lousy detective, but he's not so stupid he won't figure out Kirwin worked for the Nose. Did Kirwin tell you he talked to Red?"

Claire shook her head.

"Your old man isn't playing straight with you. We've always been honest with each other. You going to let Kirwin mess that up?

"No, I'm not," Claire said, "I should have told you."

"Damn right you should have," he said opening the car door. "I'll see what I can do, but it's for you, not your old man."

"Thanks," she called after him.

Her face flushed with embarrassment. Ever since Kirwin showed up, she'd been feeling her way along about what she was supposed to do, and now, she felt like a fool for walling out Rafe.

She needed to get her head screwed on right. A DNA connection without a lifetime of mutual support didn't earn Kirwin the right to mess up her life.

On top of feeling humiliated, she was mad. Kirwin bald-faced lied by omission when he didn't tell her Red questioned him.

And Kirwin did it right after she'd ponied up for security and a defense attorney.

Wonder if Kirwin told Red the same half-assed story he'd told her about his job with the Nose.

Jenny looked up, surprised to see Claire. "Hey, look at you. No one was expecting to see you in the office. How's Kirwin?"

"He's better, thank you. And thanks for the help finding him a lawyer."

Claire headed to her office. She felt most at home at work. She knew who she was at the office, what the expectations were, and how she fit in with the people around her. Not at all like her life at home had become.

She was hanging up her coat when Mr. Marsh buzzed her line.

"Just making sure Guthrie got in touch."

"Yes, thank you for the help."

"Sorry about your father. Take some time off if you want. I can handle anything that comes up with Amanda."

"Has she called you?"

"No," he said, "but she hasn't fired us either. Take care of yourself."

The last thing Claire wanted to do was go home and stew over Kirwin. She dug out the Tutwiler file and opened it.

Five days into the investigation and she'd hit a wall.

All investigations are like giant jigsaw puzzles with the pieces scattered on the floor.

None of the pieces of the Tutwiler case were fitting together. She took out a fresh legal pad and wrote the names of everyone connected to the Tutwiler murder, then drew arrows between them, and added notes describing their connections.

She let her eyes float lazily over the notes, just letting her mind skim over the words, looking for what she'd missed.

She couldn't find a thing.

When a case stymies, it's time to rattle the cages and kick down the doors.

She booted up her computer and went to work. Her high school English teacher called the Internet an open sewer. For Claire, it was a treasure trove of information.

She pulled up Colorado Vital Records, searching for a marriage license for David Lucas Backstrom.

Found it.

Sonja Ottilie Schmidt had been nineteen when she married Dave in Denver County. She'd been twenty when Luke was born. On Luke's birth certificate, in the box referring to *Prior live births to this mother* was typed "*1.*"

Where was Sonja's first kid?

She switched to hunting for Sonja's birth certificate. With a name like Sonja Ottilie Schmidt, it wasn't hard to find. Her birth was registered in Weld County by her father, Karl who self-identified as a rancher.

In a cue of related "Schmidt" documents, she found a second Schmidt birth certificate. At the age of fourteen, Sonja gave birth to a boy she named Jesse Otto Schmidt, but she didn't name the child's father.

Claire sat back. Jesse would be 32 years old now if

he was still alive. She searched for a death certificate in Jesse's name. Didn't find one issued for him, but Karl Schmidt had died twenty-five years ago.

Who got the ranch?

In the Colorado Land Records and Deeds, the name Schmidt didn't get a hit. When she searched Backstrom, she found it. A deed for over 400 acres was issued to Sonja Schmidt Backstrom not long after Karl Schmidt died.

Whoa, uptight little Miss Perfect Sonja had a love child and a ranch.

She wondered if Sonja kept in touch with Jesse. It would have been easy enough. Weld county was only a hundred miles up the road. But did she?

Claire commiserated with Sonja's first born. She was an expert on the pain of abandonment.

Her cell phone ringing brought her back to the moment.

The Biologics lab had the results. Luke's DNA was not a perfect match to the sample from the crime scene, but the two people were closely related.

"Not a parent," the laboratory director told her, "but perhaps a sibling."

Claire thanked him and hung up.

She considered calling Rafe to fill him in . . . but what if she was wrong? She doubted she was, and in the mood he was in, she didn't want to send him on a wild goose chase.

CHAPTER EIGHTEEN

LUKE DUMPED THE JUMBLE OF OLD PHOTOGRAPHS AND papers out of Sonja's chest onto the top of his desk. He shoved the pictures aside and picked up a bundle of rubber-banded documents.

Sonja's birth certificate was on top. He smiled when he read her birth year. She'd lopped five years off her age.

Clipped to her birth certificate was a deed transferring from the estate of Karl Otto Schmidt to Sonja Schmidt Backstrom 421 acres located in the West half of Section 31 and the Southeast quarter of Section 32 in Weld County.

He was stunned.

The stupid cow.

Why hadn't she told him about the ranch? The oil companies were fracking and drilling all over Weld County.

Shit, all their money problems could be solved.

And then he found the answer.

Four days after Dave's body had been pulled from the ravine, she penned a codicil to her will, witnessed by strangers and notarized by a woman who worked at UR Mailbox.

His head jerked back in surprise at the eye-popping sentence, *I leave my ranch in Weld County to Jesse Otto Schmidt.*

What the hell was going on? Who the fuck was Jesse Otto Schmidt? She never talked about a brother.

She was a lying sack of shit. Here he was busting his ass to support her, and she owned a ranch and someone other than him was getting it when she died.

A yellowing half-sheet of paper slipped out of the folds of the will.

Another bombshell.

He felt gut-punched and hollowed out. He read it again, and then again, thinking he was missing something. And he had.

His whole life trembled on a foundation of lies. He wasn't an only child. She wasn't just *his* mother. This Jesse Otto Schmidt was her kid, too.

The hollowed out feeling filled with anger.

What else was she hiding?

In an instant, he was on his feet pounding toward the sitting room.

Sonja looked up when Luke burst in.

"What's wrong? What's happened?"

He thrust Jesse's birth certificate in her face.

She cringed from him, a whispery moan escaping her lips.

"You have another fucking kid," he yelled. Luke dropped the holographic will in her lap. "You left him a ranch. You're a fucking fool! That whole county is bubbling in oil."

She cowered, a hand up as if she expected a blow. "Don't talk to me like that."

"What did this guy ever do for you? I take care of

you. Did he talk you into changing the will?" Luke thrust his face almost to the tip of her nose. "That's it, isn't it? He's the one you've been talking on the phone to."

His rage boiled over. "I don't even know who you are."

"I'm your Mother," she said trying to sound like she wasn't terrified.

Luke spun around. "Why does he get the ranch?"

"He lives there. He's…he's different. He gets so angry, and he can't dial it down. I thought he'd grow out of it, but . . . I can't explain it." Anger flashed across her face. "What did I know? I was a kid myself. The doctor gave him pills, but Jesse won't take them."

She got up on her feet, pleading. "Don't you see? He's not like you. He has to have the ranch."

"It's all lies, isn't it? Everything you ever told me." He looked down at the birth certificate. "You were, what, fourteen when you had him?" Luke sneered. "You and Dad didn't meet on a ski slope during spring break, did you?"

"Dave concocted that story." She turned away from him. "I met your Dad in a bar in Wildcat Springs. I never even finished high school." She turned and faced him. "I've seen to it you've led a charmed life. You have no idea how I grew up."

"How could I? You never talked about it."

Her eyes had a far-away look. "I was born twenty miles out of Wildcat Springs in a ramshackle house you wouldn't keep a dog in, and my father was the meanest —"

"Who gives a rip?" Luke shouted over her. "You got yourself a sweetheart deal when you married Dad."

"I didn't lie to him about Jesse. Dave made me promise I'd turn my back on the past."

And then she started to cry. "I couldn't do it. I loved Jesse. But don't you understand I did the right thing? It was best for Jesse to grow up on the ranch."

"Let me get this straight," Luke said. "You abandoned your son to his mean grandpa and left him to live on a ranch you couldn't wait to escape, but it was a good deal for your first-born kid? That's some damn good lying to yourself."

Sonja stiffened. "I didn't abandon him. After my Dad died, Gus and Frieda moved in the house. They get the income from the ranch in return for looking after Jesse."

Luke shoved his finger in her face. "You broke your promise to Dad."

"Don't be so judgmental. You sound like him, so self-righteous," Sonja said turning away. "You have no idea what I've been through."

"Can't blame me about that."

Sonja kept talking like she hadn't heard Luke. "Jesse's different. He gets something in his head all backwards, and then he can't stop thinking about it. He gets all churned up and when he gets like that, bad things happen."

Luke taunted. "Like what, Mom? What has my half-bro done when he's in one of his moods?"

She looked him in the eye. "He killed Tutwiler."

Luke's anger turned to shock, then he recoiled from her. "How do you know?"

"He told me."

Luke slapped his hand to his forehead. "My God, you've been lying to the police."

"I've been protecting my son. Jesse did it to 'even things up.' That's what he called it." She paused for a moment, then shouted, "He did it because he loves me. Jesse knew about the trial and Dave's suicide."

"Because you told him," Luke accused. "You got him all revved up. You unburdened yourself on a nutcase." Luke jabbed his finger in her face. "You egged him on, playing 'poor pitiful me,' so he'd kill Tutwiler for you. Hell, I've been worried you hired a hitman. You didn't have to. You have your own pet psycho."

She looked horrified. "No, no it wasn't like that. Don't call him psycho. He's my son."

"You sure as hell never treated him that way."

Sonja ignored him. "Jesse can't get into trouble. You have to help me protect him."

"Trouble? Listen to yourself. He gunned Tutwiler down in his own home." Luke was pacing, then stopped in front of her. "You have to fix this."

"What do you mean fix it?"

"He has access to a telephone and the Internet," Luke said. "There is no middle-of-nowhere anymore. One word from him when he's in one of his moods, and you're in jail. Turn him in to the cops."

"I can't turn my son into the police!"

"He's your responsibility. You take care of this mess or get his father to – or do you even know who his father is?"

Sonja didn't answer.

Luke laughed bitterly. "Oh, that's rich. You spread your legs for every cowboy in the county."

She shook her head. "No…"

"Tell me," he jeered. "Tell me you know who the father is."

A low growl came from the back of Sonja's throat.

Then it dawned on Luke. It was like the hollowed-out feeling doubled in size.

"Your father is Jesse's dad. That's why he's all fucked up."

She clutched his forearm, digging her nails into his skin.

"No, no . . ." she whimpered, "it's not like that. I have to keep my Jesse safe."

Luke pried her fingers off his arm. "Really, you're going to aid and abet a felon? Get real mother, you're not thinking straight."

She shook her head, knowing what he was going to demand.

"Call the cops."

"Jesse can't go to prison. When he gets around people, he acts crazy."

"He is crazy!" Luke shouted. He fished his phone out of his pocket. "Call them or I will."

"How could you? He's your brother."

Luke shook his head. "He's your bastard."

Sonja flung the phone across the room. "Dave could be cold like that—so hard and cold."

"Don't badmouth Dad. You chose him over Jesse. I'm not going down with you. Your decision Mom— what are you going to do?"

"I'm going to the ranch and do what I should have done all these years. Help my boy."

"What's your plan? Hide him in the trunk of your car and sneak into Canada? You're already an accessory to a crime. Stop while you're ahead."

"Shut up," she hissed. "You ungrateful prick. I kept all the ugliness from ever touching your life." She turned and left the room, clattering down the stairs.

He called after her, "You fucked that up, too."

Luke heard the whine of the garage door going up.

No damaged half-bro was messing up his plans. The ranch was his birthright and any oil under the dirt was his, too.

He grabbed his car keys.

CHAPTER NINETEEN

Luke pulled into the only gas station and convenience store in Wildcat Springs. The town boasted a single street with a tiny post office, a hardware store, and a Five-and-Dime. Half a dozen pickups, all dirty and banged-up, were parked around the only café. A sprinkling of houses in desperate need of paint lined the other side of the road. He could throw a rock from one end of town to the other, and probably hit a cow just outside the city limits.

He had passed plenty of oil tankers and water trucks on the highway, but the oil boom hadn't reached this god-forsaken town.

Luke parked at the gas pumps and locked the Porsche. Wind gusts were knocking the wind chill into near-winter levels. *What were the advantages of living here?*

"Nice ride, Mister," the kid behind the counter said. He never took his eyes off the Porsche. If a topless woman walked by, it could be a toss-up which way the boy would look.

Luke had to tap his keys on the counter to get the

kid to finally shake his attention from the car and swivel his head toward Luke. "Help you with something?"

"I'm looking for the Schmidt ranch."

"Old man Schmidt done passed," the kid said.

Luke nodded his head. "Yeah, I know, but do you know how to get to the ranch?"

"Sure." The kid gave directions, complete with pointing and hand gestures. "Veer right at the second field with a herd grazing, go down a ways, then take the left turn before the boulder field."

Luke slid money across the counter for the gas and returned to the Porsche. Two boys had their hands cupped on the windows and their faces pressed to the glass. They jumped on their bikes when they saw Luke coming and pedaled like the devil was after them.

He pumped gas, then drove north out of town and when he saw a pile of rocks, he took the turn, and the Porsche shimmied over the cattle guard onto a dirt road littered with stones. He followed the road through a pasture of cow dung dotted with tufts of dry grass grazed to short nubs.

He rounded a curve and idled at the top of a low rise. Spread out below him on a flat plain was an old rock house with smoke coming out of the chimney. A barn older than dirt sat north of the house and looked rickety enough that he figured a good gust of wind would lift the roof off and send it to Nebraska. Two farm sheds listing away from the prevailing winds were by a corral with three horses hanging their heads low. Even the animals were depressed.

The whole place looked worn out and used up. Whatever income Gus and Frieda got was barely enough to keep a roof over their heads.

Sonja's gray Mercedes was angled in by the porch of the ranch house.

The Porsche fishtailed down the incline, rumbling to a stop by her car.

The moment he killed the engine, the front screen door banged open, and a heavy-set older man stepped out on the porch. He stood with his legs spread and his arms hanging loosely at his sides.

Luke got out of the car.

"Can I help you?" The man's voice was deep and not very friendly.

"Sure," Luke said, leaning on his front fender with his arms crossed over his chest. "I'm Luke Backstrom."

Sonja flew out of the house, the screen door banging behind her. "I'll handle this Gus."

Gus ignored her and stepped off the porch, moving toward Luke. "What do you want?"

Sonja was right on his heels.

Luke tilted his head and scratched behind his ear. "To meet my bro."

"Go home Luke." Sonja begged. "This has nothing to do with you."

"Yeah, it does. You made it my business."

Sonja turned to Gus. "He's here for Jesse. He knows."

Gus looked perplexed.

A gray-haired woman with an apron tied around her waist came out on the porch. "Gus? What's going on?"

Luke smiled. "Jesse killed Morgan Tutwiler."

A rail-thin cowboy stepped out on the porch.

Gus hollered. "Frieda, go on back in the house and take Jesse with you."

Sonja screamed, "No, Jesse, get in the car. Now!"

Jesse ran down the porch steps to Gus. "What's going on?" He jerked his head toward Luke. "Who's he?"

Sonja had her car doors standing open. "Jesse come

here. I'll explain it to you on the way." Her voice ratcheting towards hysterical, "Gus, help me! He won't live if they send him to prison!"

Frieda walked to Gus and Jesse and pointed at Sonja. "Get in your fancy car and leave. We'll take care of our boy."

She elbowed Gus in the ribs. "You old fool. I have eyes in my head. I know he's your son."

Then as if on some sort of silent cue, all five of them turned towards the sound of a car racing down the hill.

<hr>

BUG BARRELED down the slope toward the ranch house, spewing dust out behind his wheels. He slalomed to flat ground, shuddering to a stop in the yard. It would have been comical under other circumstances.

Claire had her phone to her ear, yelling to Rafe, "Schmidt Ranch! Weld County," as she jumped out of the car and ran toward the group standing stock still with their mouths gaping.

"Frieda, get back in the house," the old man yelled.

Luke ran over to Claire and grabbed her arm. "What are you doing here?"

Her feet scrabbled underneath her like she was doing a soft-shoe in the sand. She caught her balance and tried to pull her arm away.

Luke yanked her around, pinning her to his chest and wrenching her arm up high and tight behind her back.

Claire kicked out trying to strike a blow to his knees, but he was too fast.

He slapped his hand over her mouth and pinched her nose closed with his thumb and forefinger.

She stared at the others, wondering why they were

frozen in place watching him try to kill her. She flailed at him, but he was stronger. Her lungs were on fire, and she saw stars and heard a roaring in her ears.

She went limp, bending toward the ground like a broken branch, forcing Luke to bear her weight.

He overbalanced and lost his grip on her mouth.

She chomped down hard on his palm, grinding the flesh between her teeth.

Luke let loose a garbled curse and let go of her, raining down blows on her head with his good hand.

She hung on like a bulldog, ripping at his flesh.

Luke's punches brought new stars—bigger, brighter.

But she must have literally struck a nerve as he howled and thrust her away.

Claire fell backward on her rear and rolled away from him. But he was on her in a flash.

His vicious kick to her head stunned her.

She wrapped her arms around her head.

He kept after her, delivering a walloping kick to her ribs.

She braced herself for another attack, but the old man flung himself at Luke, knocking him to the ground.

The two of them rolled in the dirt, clawing and hollering.

Claire pulled herself to her hands and knees, trying to suck in air.

Sonja was still yelling to Jesse to come with her. Claire saw Frieda's hand disappear into her apron.

Frieda pulled a gun and pointed it at Sonja. "He's my boy. He ain't going anywhere with you."

Gus rolled off Luke, who stayed down on the ground. He yelled, "Freida, no!"

Jesse launched himself at Frieda; she fired before she went flying into the dirt.

Jesse jumped to his feet and ran to Sonja.

Gus scrambled over to Frieda and pulled her head into his lap.

And Luke was belly-crawling to the gun.

Claire stood swaying on her feet. The whack on her head had her seeing double the stars, and everything else.

There were two Jesses holding Sonja. Two Lukes pointing the pistol at Jesse.

"Get away from my mother!" Luke yelled.

Jesse jumped to his feet snarling like an animal. His roundhouse punch caught Luke on the jaw and sent him reeling.

Luke toppled over on his back, the gun flying out of his hands.

Claire pulled the gun from the back of her waistband. "Everyone get your hands up where I can see them."

They looked at her as if they had forgotten she was there, then Luke raised his hands.

Gus and Frieda hoisted theirs.

But Jesse was screaming at Luke, "She's my mom! Mine!"

Sirens howled, and two Sheriff's vehicles sped over the ridge.

Jesse turned and ran for Sonja's car.

CHAPTER TWENTY

A week after Morgan Tutwiler's murder, Claire was waiting in Mr. Marsh's office. Her ribs were still taped, and breathing brought uncomfortable memories of Luke Backstrom's foot. Worse, she had a lump the size of a hen's egg on her head and the bruising spread from her hairline all the way down to her chin, staining her face a mottled blue and purple.

At least her skull wasn't fractured, but considering how awful she looked, she might have made that trade. As long as she didn't make any sudden moves, the pain was manageable.

Marsh hurried in. "Sorry I'm late." As he passed by her, he put his hand on her shoulder.

She winced.

He jerked his hand back. "Oh. Sorry. How are you doing?"

"Plenty sore, but I'm going to be okay."

Marsh rounded his desk and sat down. She slid her report in front of him. He picked it up and flipped through the pages and tossed it aside.

"This is great for the files, but I'd rather just hear it from you."

"There's a warrant out for Jesse's arrest, but no one knows where he is. Rafe has both the Colorado and Wyoming Highway Patrol looking for him. He's thinking of adding the FBI if something doesn't come up soon. They found Sonja's Mercedes dumped near Red Feather Lakes. He might have hitchhiked out of that area, or just hiked. He'll be hard to find. Jesse's been disappearing into the wilderness and living off the land since he was a kid. If he makes it to the Bridger-Teton Wilderness, he'll have nearly four million acres and three mountain ranges to hide in."

"They'll catch him when he surfaces for something he needs. Winter's coming, and even the best survivalists need a ton of provisions to survive in the wilderness."

Claire shook her head. It hurt, so she told herself to stop doing that.

"I don't know. The early mountain men stayed out there for decades. Sonja's hired him a top criminal attorney and another for herself. She's sitting in jail, charged with aiding and abetting a felon and obstruction of justice. She can't make bail, so I don't know how she can afford her lawyer."

"Did you press charges against Luke?"

"I did. He tried to kill me."

"He should be sent up. Shouldn't be an issue there. Are you sending your medical bills to Jenny like we agreed?"

"I am, thank you." Claire shifted in the chair, looking for a pain-free way to sit. "Is Amanda still our client?"

Marsh grinned. "Yes, she is. She and James plan to marry as soon as the ink dries on his divorce papers, and they're planning to honeymoon in Paris."

Claire resisted shaking her head. Poor Amanda, she deserved better, but the firm would be around to pick up the pieces. And there would be pieces.

"At least the firm doesn't have to hunt for a new client to replace her."

"I'm always on the lookout for a rainmaker like Tutwiler. I can't let this firm's future rest on the whims of one young woman. Hey," he paused, then asked, "Why don't you take some time off and go someplace warm? Get some rest; you went above and beyond."

"I'd rather just putter around the house. Kirwin's still in the VA hospital getting therapy for his hand. When he's released, he'll have to get a place of his own."

"Have you told him he has to move?"

"I did, and it felt pretty good. Abe Guthrie got him squared away with the police, and the place he was working for over on Speer agreed to take him back."

"Glad it worked out for him. Let me know if you need anything—and don't let me see you in the office anytime soon."

Claire thanked him and rose to her feet slowly. Trying to get out of a chair without jostling her sore ribs was something she hadn't yet mastered.

She paused in front of Marsh's desk.

"Next time anything involving someone named 'Tutwiler' comes up, maybe think twice about calling me in on it." She tried to smile. "They seem to be hazardous to my health."

Marsh nodded. "You got it."

She made it down to the garage. On top of her other challenges, like walking and blinking, driving was no picnic either.

———

Claire unlocked her front door and headed to the bathroom. She shook out two Advil tablets and washed them down with a glass of water.

There was an unopened bottle of Riesling she'd been saving to celebrate the end of the case. She grabbed the wine out of the otherwise nearly empty refrigerator, and went into the living room and sank into a chair.

It felt wonderful to be home, no phone ringing, no stressing over a case . . . just peace and silence, and nothing on the horizon.

She leaned back and rested her head on the chair, closed her eyes and gave herself over to the Advil. She could feel the pain draining out of her body. Finally.

She was half-asleep when her phone rang. She opened one eye and glanced down. Of all people, she would answer for him.

"How are you feeling?" Rafe asked.

"Better than yesterday, and hopefully better tomorrow."

"I wanted to thank you for saving my ass on the Tutwiler case. Without you, the case might be unsolved."

"You would have figured it out. I owe you for helping Guthrie square things for Kirwin," she said. "How's your family?"

"Good. Di's sticking with rehab, and Lily's happy."

There was a long pause, and she knew whatever came next would be the real reason he called.

"Hey, I got a question for you. How did the Biologics Lab happen to have a sample of Luke's DNA?"

She paused just enough to make it sound like she was thinking. "He must have been researching his ancestry."

"Really? Who ordered a comparison of his DNA to the Tutwiler killer's sample?"

"I have no idea what goes on in scientific laboratories." Which was true but didn't answer his question.

"Uh huh." She could almost hear him smiling. "You get to feeling better and we'll have a beer and talk about it some more. Until then, take care of yourself."

"I will."

Now, she was wide awake.

She put her phone down, topped off her wine and put her feet up on the coffee table to think.

Jesse might never be caught and punished for murdering Tutwiler, but most of the time, life has a way of evening up the score. Even if it amounted to looking over his shoulder and living in a tent through the mountain winters with only his guilt to keep him company, that would be its own punishment.

Both Sonja and Luke were suffering, which brought her no concern. They earned their pain. The Millennium Construction Company and the Backstrom family home were both up for sale, and the proceeds would enrich the criminal defense attorneys they couldn't otherwise afford.

Sonja and Frieda were grieving the loss of their child, and for that, Claire's heart ached too. Perhaps the pain from the loss of a child was borne by all women.

The emotional fallout from Sonja's secret would ripple through the family for the rest of their lives.

The truth might set you free, but first it will break your heart.

Why was she demanding Kirwin spill his guts?

His past belonged to him. If she kept poking through her family's history, she might stumble on something she couldn't look away from—and didn't want to know.

She made a deal with herself to quit asking Kirwin to talk about his life with Eleanor and how they lived in Chicago, and who they knew and what they did. She realized there would be no positive side to whatever he had to say. Her parents left her; the *whys* didn't matter.

She and Kirwin needed a fresh start. To leave the past alone and let the future unfold. There was always hope with new beginnings. The deadweight of history didn't need to tag along.

Claire pulled the throw closer around her and rested her head on the chair, closing her eyes and thinking how still the house was, how quiet it was without anyone else there. How quickly she had become accustomed to the noise and energy of having someone in the house.

She had gone through more than half a bottle of wine on an empty stomach when she decided a puppy would be sweet to come home to. A dog wouldn't be much trouble, and he'd be so happy to see her when she opened the front door.

After living with Kirwin for six days, a puppy would be easy-peasy, right?

UNSPEAKABLE GRUDGES

Chapter 1

The girl at the end of the bar was a perfect specimen. Cupid lips with red gloss. Pert little body all tight and toned. A crop top showed a flat belly, and a silver ring piercing her navel. Long legs and a nice ass in a pair of worn Wranglers made him hard. He couldn't not stare.

She noticed and batted her eyes, propping her chin on her hand. Then she slowly sucked on her little finger while watching his reaction. A seductive smile broadened into a grin, and she strolled over to him.

"You lookin' for company, cowboy?"

He nodded without taking his gaze off her.

She sat on the stool next to him and brushed against him, making him even harder.

This woman would be even easier once he flashed enough cash and a baggie of coke.

See, boy, his mother chided in his head, *it'll be easy, even for a loser like you.*

The bartender approached and pointed at the bar, silently asking if they wanted another.

He nodded, and a few moments later, two frosty bottles were in front of them. She favored a fruity beer that smelled like apricots, and the bartender kept them coming. The more she drank, the more she fawned over him, hanging on his every word.

There were only two other customers in the place, both old men looking like they had nowhere else to go. Country music played from overhead speakers, but no one was listening.

They chatted about nothing, and she giggled way too much. She grabbed the bottle -- her third or fourth -- and when she drank, beer dribbled from her lips, leaving tiny golden teardrops on her breasts.

He squirmed on the bar stool.

This woman needed punishing.

"You haven't told me your name, sweet thang." She batted her eyes again, one fake eyelash springing like a coil from her eyelid.

"Clint. You?"

"You can call me Tiger. You interested in a private party?"

He smiled. Just another buckle bunny hanging in a dive near the Denver stockyards, hoping to hook up with a cowboy and spend his cash.

"You ready to ride?" she asked, wiping her mouth with the back of her hand. She managed to get off the barstool without falling but stumbled on the way to the door. She grabbed a chair to keep herself from sprawling on the floor.

He threw a couple of bills on the bar, got his leather coat, and sauntered out after her, watching her sweet little ass sway.

His thing was bull riding. He earned his pro ticket by busting his ass on every bull near his hometown of Stephenville, Texas. Willing buckle bunnies like Tiger sweetened the rewards, and this one would help him atone for his sin.

I'm nearly cleansed, Lord. My time to be with You is soon.

Clint caught up with her on the sidewalk outside the Kickin' Ass Bar and cupped her tight little bottom.

She wiggled her rear against his hand, and he knew this would be easy. Too easy.

"You stayin' near here?" she asked, slurring a little.

The flashing pink neon sign of the bar -- a kicking mule -- cast soft light on her pretty face.

"Walk with me, babe," he said, deliberately sounding drunk even though he wasn't. "I like how them hips move."

He guided her to the end of the block, where the streetlights were spaced farther apart, several broken out, providing the darkness he craved.

She snuggled under his arm. "Where you takin' me?"

He took in the scent of her cheap perfume. "You'll see. Ain't far, and we'll have a good ride."

He kept her upright for two more blocks, past shuttered storefronts, to the end of the pavement. Across an expanse of rough ground was a rusted, corrugated metal building. Now empty of hay, the three-sided shed would give them enough privacy.

She tossed her empty bottle into the weeds. He handed her his beer. She threw her head back and chugged it, lost her balance, and staggered.

He pulled her tightly to him. "I think you're 'bout ready to party."

She looked up, excitement sparkling on her face.

He backed her up several steps until she was well inside the shed, and then pushed her gently to the ground. He straddled her, then lowered his body onto hers.

Her chin jutted up expectantly, and she puckered her lips for a kiss. Her hand slid up his thigh.

"Come on cowboy, show me what you got in those Levi's."

He grabbed both wrists and tugged her arms above her head.

She squirmed and tossed her head away from him, frowning. "I don't like it rough."

He planted a hard kiss on her lips, and she relaxed beneath him, dropping her guard. It gave him the chance to slip the kerchief from around his neck. When he pulled his lips away from hers, he jammed it into her mouth.

That was when terror bloomed in her eyes.

She tried to throw him off, but he outweighed her.

He leaned down close to her left ear.

"We're gonna play a game -- the Eight Second Game. Just like I gotta stay on the bull eight seconds to get a score, you got eight seconds to tell me why you deserve to live. I'm gonna take the gag out of your mouth. You're not gonna yell, or I'll snap your neck."

He kept his hand over her mouth and squeezed until she struggled to breathe.

"Understand?"

There was a moan. It might have been a yes.

He pulled out the gag, keeping one hand firmly on her throat, the other stretching her arms far above her head.

"One . . . two . . ."

"Because -- because --"

"Three . . ."

Her eyes widened with fear. She struggled for a deep breath, but he scooted forward, seating himself directly over her lungs, pushing the air out of her.

"Four . . . five . . ."

"Baby -- gotta child," she wheezed.

"You with the kid's father?"

"No." She gasped.

"Six . . ."

She tried to get purchase with her legs to buck him, but he was heavy and bulked with muscle.

"Seven . . ."

"My b-baby needs me . . ."

"He needs a family, you bitch. Eight."

He shifted his weight, and she sucked in a lungful of air.

She tried to raise her hips, but she was no match.

He stuffed the rag back in her mouth.

Lord? It's me, Aaron. This gal is my sin offering.

He looked down into her terrified eyes and sang in a little kid sing-song voice: "The Lord is waiting to meet you, to meet you, to meet you . . ."

Her screams were muffled.

He slipped his hand inside his jacket.

She struggled to twist her arms out of his hand at the same time she raised her hips, but she had weakened.

"Be still. You're laying on the Lord's altar."

He whipped out a short truncheon and raised it above her face, so she could see it, so she could anticipate the arc of the descent.

The first blow knocked her unconscious.

The second blow smashed the cartilage in her nose and crumpled her cheekbone on the left side of her pretty face, but she still looked like his Ma.

He struck again and again. Blood spattered the weeds.

His arm grew weary and his breath ragged by the time he looked down at her with satisfaction. Her face was unrecognizable.

Out of his pearl-button shirt pocket, he withdrew a

pinch of finely ground incense and sprinkled it over her ruined face in the sign of the cross.

"You can't sin no more, and your blood washes away my sin."

He whipped out his pocket knife and cut off the ring finger of her left hand, sliding it into the back pocket of his jeans.

He stood above her, a foot on either side of her body.

A quick look around satisfied him the area was deserted and silent.

He straightened her legs and crossed her hands over her stomach.

A light, cold rain fell as he gathered a few bedraggled oxeye daisy blooms and tucked them into her hands. Then he walked off at a fast clip to his pickup stashed in a leaning run-in shed that hadn't housed a horse in years.

In the vehicle were plastic bags for his bloody clothes and a pair of fresh jeans and a shirt. He got naked and, just as God had commanded Aaron to cleanse himself after he made sacrifices on the Day of Atonement, Clint toweled off with bottled water and wiped the blood spatter from his boots before he put on the fresh clothes.

See Lord, no mistakes. I was smarter with this one.

He headed for the Night's Rest Motel, a rattletrap tourist court from the 1940's with two rows of ramshackle cabins forming a half-moon around a potholed parking lot.

He whistled as he put the truck in park and smiled when he stepped out into the cool night air in front of the motel office.

His mama had always said he would come to no good, claiming he was like his father, meaner than a snake and crazy.

You see what I done, Ma? Won't be long till I'm atoned for my sin.

"Hey, you!" a voice yelled at him. "Clint Barlow! Get outta here. You done tore up the room the last time you stayed here."

The owner of the motel stood outside the office smoking a cigarette. His comb-over blew in the breeze, standing straight up in long thin wisps before settling like a half-built bird's nest on his scalp. He flicked his cigarette onto the pavement and ground it out with his boot. Had his hands on his hips as Clint approached.

"Lookee here," Clint said. "Earl Allen Jacoby. You still alive?"

"You got eyes, doncha boy?"

"I got money, old man. Keep your britches on."

"And doncha call me Earl Allen. You call me my rodeo name -- Wild Dog. I earned it."

"You old bastard, you ain't rode a pony on a carnival carousel in thirty years. Your bronc bustin' days were over before I got born." Clint pulled a few bills out of his wallet and waved them at Wild Dog.

At the sight of the money, Wild Dog turned and hobbled into the office.

Clint followed into an over-heated room with peeling paint and brown-edged posters advertising long past events. The place never changed. Always smelled of the greasy food Wild Dog fried up.

Wild Dog's rubber-soled shoes made sticky sounds as he crossed the dirty vinyl floor to the desk. He sat on his stool and pulled himself closer to the countertop. He held out one hand, making the *gimme* gesture to Clint.

With the other hand, he shoved the dog-eared guest register across the desk.

"Fifty-two dollars. Cash."

Clint counted out the cash. He slid the money over and then scribbled his name in the beaten-up book.

Wild Dog clutched the cash with one hand and gave Clint an old-fashioned metal room key with the other. "You're in early tonight," he said. "Couldn't score any tail, huh?" Clint reached over the counter, seized Wild Dog by the throat and shook him until his glasses fell off.

"Don't insult me, old man. I ain't payin' you a dime for the room." Clint gave him one final shake before grabbing the cash.

Wild Dog gave a half nod and slid his hand along the top of the cracked Formica.

Clint reached over the counter and got there before Wild Dog did, yanking out the shotgun. He racked the slide of the twelve-gauge.

"Always liked this piece."

Wild Dog backed up to the wall behind him.

"Didn't mean no harm. It's cool man. I need my gun. You know how it is here. Gimme my gun."

A smile flitted across Clint's face. "Naw. I'm keeping it. And you know what?"

Wild Dog shook his head.

"Anyone asks you when I came in tonight, you tell them you saw me go into my room before five o'clock and not come out."

"Why would I do that? You cheated me out of the room rent and stole my gun."

"Because you screwed the Kingpin outta his cut of that last load of coke, and if a little bird tells him, he'll cut your throat."

Wild Dog's face paled, and he held up his hands in surrender. "Okay, man. Take the gun."

"And I was in my room by five, right?"

"Yeah, I swear. You was in by five." He cocked his head towards the window. "What happened out there?"

"How would I know? I been asleep in my room all evening."

Clint strolled out with the shotgun slung over his shoulder.

CHAPTER 2

THE DJ WARNED OF A CRASH AT THE ENTRANCE RAMP TO Interstate 25, but at the rate she was going, the tow truck driver would be having lunch before she got there. The torrential rain didn't help, and probably caused the accident.

If she was late to her first meeting, her launch of Claire Callahan, Private Investigator might be over before it officially started. Marsh & Whitley, LLP may be understanding of a traffic snarl, but the important client they wanted her to meet may not be so forgiving.

A new song came on, and she took her eyes off the rain-drenched road to glance at the thick, black clouds gathering on the horizon.

It just isn't getting any better.

As if to confirm this, the DJ interrupted the song, warning that the rising waters of the Platte River threatened the closure of the bridges, including the Alameda Bridge near downtown Denver. If that happened, she'd need to find another route to get on I-25. That would guarantee she'd be late.

She gripped the wheel of her Volkswagen Bug,

thinking about how proud Grandma Callie would be of her. Though her parents dumped Claire on Callie's front porch and then disappeared, Callie had taken her and raised her—and Claire grew up to be the spitting image of her grandmother when she was a young woman -- tall, redheaded, and stubborn as a mule.

You'll get there, don't freak out. With any luck the proposed client will be even later.

Landing a contract to provide investigative services to a major law firm like Marsh & Whitely would give her a leg up, and money from this gig would tide her over until she could add to her client list. Well, if she had a client list. With her savings drained and credit card nearly maxed out, she needed to impress Mr. Marsh.

After eighteen months training with a private investigator at the Davis Law Firm, she'd passed the licensing exam and struck out on her own. She'd made her share of gaffes, but she'd honed her skills and learned some pretty salty language to boot.

She trained under a retired Irish cop, Mac McNally, a private eye with the Davis Law Firm. Without his recommendation, she wouldn't have landed this new job. She was ready . . . if she wasn't turned away before she got to the meeting room.

During her training, she'd pursued an ex-husband suspected of killing his six-year-old daughter, and found enough evidence for Rafe Brewster, a detective with Denver's Sixth Division, to step in and make the arrest. Cops needed a warrant. She didn't. He was impressed, and she made an important friend.

A light went off as if someone took her picture, and a moment later, thunder exploded overhead. The thick smell of ozone filtered through Bug's asthmatic heater.

A row of red taillights stretched before her. As she

crept toward the Alameda Bridge, the normally placid river was racing over the bridge and raging between the bridge struts, creating white caps in the brown water. The car in front of her slowed to make an awkward U-turn and backtrack west. She followed suit and joined the line of commuters running from the rising Platte River.

A detour led her across the Platte and once she crossed the Sixth Street Bridge, traffic thinned. She released her death grip on the wheel. She was on the same side of the river as her new job.

Marsh and Whitely, Attorneys at Law, purchased a historically-significant building as a project and created office space that made their legal competitors green with envy. The firm's reputation as hard-working straight-shooters was now mirrored in a prestigious headquarters -- stone-faced and oozing style.

She had wanted to be a lawyer once, but her plans for pursuing a career in law died the same summer her grandmother had. Alone in the world, she decided she had a choice: Hide under the covers or get out of bed and finish college and find a job.

Claire turned onto East Union Avenue and pulled into the parking garage of the imposing three-story office building with the original ornate bow windows marching across the facade in perfect symmetry. She made her way to the carved double doors covered by a portico and entered the lobby.

Reception and record archives were located on the first floor while the associates toiled in cubicles on the second, dreaming of making partner and ascending to the third floor where the big bucks were made. Exactly where she was headed.

On the ride up, she tucked her white shirt into her best pair of black pants, an outfit she'd bought in a resale shop. Once she had whittled down the balance on her student debt, she'd be able to buy new clothes and maybe even some decent furniture for the apartment.

Hoping she looked more confident than she felt, she stepped into a large open space lined on two sides with private offices and conference rooms. The west wall was floor-to-ceiling glass, showcasing a view of downtown with the Rockies as the backdrop. The walls were a soft gray and the luxury leather furniture, and the oil paintings made an impressive show sure to wow the big money clients.

Mr. Marsh's legal assistant, Jenny, looked up from her desk. "You okay? Several people are stranded at home."

At least no one could fault her for being late if some of the employees hadn't even made it in.

"I'm fine, thank you."

"He's waiting for you in the smaller conference room." Jenny winked and gave a nod of encouragement.

"Thanks." She remembered the room from her interview. This time there wouldn't be six sets of eyes boring into her.

After turning a familiar corner, she found it. Charles Marsh sat at the table, looking every bit the elder statesman of the Denver legal community.

Though Marsh was bald, slightly overweight and shorter than Claire, his presence had such gravitas and his voice was so commanding, he drew clients who were willing to bet their bank accounts and their freedom on his talents.

She walked in, and he stood with his hand out.

"Good morning, Ms. Callahan. Would you like some coffee?"

They shook.

"No, thank you. I'm fine. I apologize for being late. The Alameda Bridge was closed."

Marsh walked over to the coffee bar. "One side of the bridge collapsed less than an hour ago."

Claire sucked in her breath.

"Was anyone hurt?"

"The first responders are still fishing people out of the water, but they aren't talking about fatalities yet." He turned around and raised one eyebrow. "Bridges that have passed inspection don't just fall down. There will be an investigation and lawsuits. We might get a piece of the business. Could put a little change in your pocket, too." He brought his coffee to the head of the table.

Claire had been standing, not sure if she should sit while he fixed his coffee or wait for his invitation.

He motioned for her to take a chair. "With the Alameda Bridge in the river, you'll have a messy commute for a long time."

The conference room door opened, and a well-built man strode in, taking a seat beside Marsh and directly across from her.

"Claire, this is Tug McLennan. Tug's a new lawyer with the firm. Mark my words, he's partner material."

McLennan looked a little surprised at the praise but managed to nod and smile at his new boss.

Tall, blond, with high cheekbones and the waspy look of an Ivy Leaguer, Tug McLennan was too young to have had any legal experience except a clerkship between the second and third year of school. Along with his expensive suit and shoes, she guessed he brought powerful family connections to the firm. She just hoped he wouldn't be hard for a girl like her to work with.

Claire, not paying attention, missed Marsh's brief monologue. Her focus snapped back just as he said: "Will that work for you two?"

Heat rose to her face as mild panic clenched her chest.

"We'll be happy to work the Tutwiler case," Tug said, covering for her.

Marsh nodded. "Good. Tutwiler is our most lucrative client. He rose to power on the back of his late wife's fortune, and he's a ruthless businessman. Tutwiler Industries is the umbrella term for a number of diverse companies, all bringing in vast streams of revenue to Tutwiler, and we want to keep our hand in his till."

Claire pulled a legal pad and pen from her bag while Marsh took a sip of coffee.

"We've been retained to represent him in his divorce," he continued. "His wife is going after him like a pit bull. It was a short second marriage that produced no children. Tutwiler wants it over quickly, but also wants his estate intact. Ms. Callahan, your job is to find the leverage he needs to eviscerate any claim on his assets by his wife. I want you to find enough dirt on Sara Tutwiler that she'll be begging to sign the mediation agreement we draw up. I also want the client in one piece when this is over. Keep him safe."

Claire nodded. "No problem."

"I'd also like to change our working agreement. Take you into the firm as our full-time investigator. I've drawn up the contract. I think you'll be pleased with the salary and the benefits package. Unless you'd rather work independently, on a per-diem basis."

She shook her head. "Absolutely not."

She tried not to look excited. Half an hour earlier, Claire worried she might be turned away due to tardiness, and now she had salaried work and full benefits.

"Good." He nodded with satisfaction. "Jenny will

show you to your office when we are finished here." Marsh turned his attention to Tug. "You'll be my second chair at Tutwiler's mediation. It's your job -- both of you -- to keep him happy. Hold his hand. Listen to the son of a bitch vent. I know it's crap work, but Morgan Tutwiler is our rainmaker. His businesses generate over two million dollars of billable hours a year for us." He glanced at his watch. "He will be here shortly to meet you."

He slid a file across the table. "Here are my case notes."

Claire took the file. "I'll be up to speed before he gets here."

Marsh turned back to McLennan. "Tug, glad-hand him and let him know you're the face of the firm. Then finish the Strayhan contracts -- he'll be in this afternoon to talk with you." Marsh stood and picked up his coffee. "Let me know if you need anything." And with that, he left.

Tug walked around the table and sat down beside her. "May I see the file?"

"Sure. What do you know about working a high-profile divorce?"

"Nothing yet, but I'm game to learn. Have you done this before?"

Claire nodded. "Yeah, I find it's best if you act as his lawyer and you don't ask questions about how I find out what I know."

WHEN THEY FINISHED READING the case file, Claire sat back in her chair. "Looks like Tutwiler thinks his wife is having an affair, but he'll need proof to force her to sign his settlement offer."

"How are you going to find out she's cheating?" Tug asked.

"I need circumstantial proof, evidence of opportunity and inclination for adultery to have occurred, but I don't have much time." She tapped the notes. "Tutwiler's mediation date is set."

"I can ask for a change of date."

They were interrupted when Jenny knocked on the conference room door and stuck in her head. "Mr. Tutwiler is here."

A moment later, Morgan Tutwiler pushed open the door and strode past Jenny carrying a bag. He was in his late fifties, round-shouldered and stooped. His mousy brown hair wasn't quite a comb-over, but it was close. The expensive Italian suit, manicured nails, and fine leather loafers were window dressing. His red-veined nose outed him as man who liked his drink.

Claire and Tug stood and introduced themselves.

Tutwiler nodded and took the seat at the head of the table.

His jowls quivered. "I want this done fast, and I don't care how you do it. That bitch is sleeping around and moaning she deserves a fat settlement. She doesn't. We've been married less than two years, and she brought nothing into the marriage. My firm hired her as a data entry clerk three years ago. She's half my age, and . . . I know I made a mistake. But, by God, I thought I loved that woman. She acted like the sweetest little gal, but the bitch was really playing me. I'm giving her a bare-knuckle fight if that's what it takes to get rid of her."

Tug glanced at Claire.

"Mr. Tutwiler," Claire said, "I'll find the proof if she's cheating, but there's no use in obtaining evidence that wouldn't be admissible in court."

"I don't care whether it's admissible in court or not.

If I'm cutting a deal with this whore, this whole shitstorm stops right here. I want you to find something that will make her look like the slut she is. You understand? Just do it."

He issued orders like he was talking to the hired help. Claire bit back a sharp retort realizing she *was* his hired help.

"What makes you think she is sleeping around?" Claire asked.

"She goes up to my family's cabin in the mountains near Evergreen. She says it's her little place to be alone and do her writing. Writing, my ass. The only thing she writes is big checks on my accounts. She's cheating on me up there."

"Is there anyone you suspect?"

"Hell, I don't know. I run a business conglomerate. I'm not home sipping hot toddies by the fire. I don't know who she sees or where she goes."

He opened his jacket pocket, took out a piece of paper, and slapped it on the table.

"There's the deed for the property in Evergreen. My signature. Right there. She's screwing around on a property I own. Get it?"

"Yes, you control access," Claire said. "I'll still need your written permission to be on the property."

"McLennan, you draft it," Tutwiler said.

Claire slide the paper over to Tug. He wrote the address down and recited it out loud. "Thirty-Seven Elk Run Ridge, Evergreen. I'll take care of it."

He excused himself and left the conference room.

Claire tapped her pencil on the legal pad in front of her. "How about computer use? Do you share a computer with your wife?"

Tutwiler reached inside the bag. "Here's her laptop. She left it in the bedroom."

"Did she buy it?"

"No, I bought it and loaned it to her. She abandoned it on my property. She has no expectation of privacy after leaving it."

Claire smiled. "Sounds like advice from a good attorney."

"I got the best, right here in the firm. The password is her mother's first name, Louise. Take it apart if you need to."

"Thank you," Claire said. "I'll need the names of her friends and a list of her family members. Also, the numbers of credit cards she has access to, the numbers of any joint bank accounts, and her full name and social security number."

He pointed at the bag with the laptop. "Sara Jenkins is her maiden name. There's a folder in there with the everything you need to know."

"Mr. Tutwiler, don't tell anyone -- not a friend, not an associate, not anyone -- that you have hired an investigator. People are most likely to have affairs with friends and colleagues."

Tutwiler stood and headed for the door. "Done. One more thing. I have a twenty-one-year-old daughter, Amanda. Leave her out of it. She's been through too much already, what with losing her mom." He paused. "I want a progress report by midday tomorrow," he said before he strode out of the conference room the same way he came in.

BOOKS BY P.H. TURNER

Winterkill
Death & Desire
Desert Heat
No Reason to Hide
Unspeakable Grudges
Secrets and Lies

ABOUT THE AUTHOR

P.H. Turner writes mystery and crime fiction set in the mountains and canyons of the West where she grew up and spent most of her working life. Pat worked in broadcast journalism on both coasts, the Midwest, and the Rocky Mountains. With roots to a Texas farm homesteaded in the 1850s, she's returned to live within miles of the old farm.

Pat is a member of Sisters in Crime and Mystery Writers of America.

P.H. Turner
www.phturner.com

www.ingramcontent.com/pod-product-compliance
Lightning Source LLC
Chambersburg PA
CBHW021648110726
47902CB00007B/1869